The Bracelet of Grood

Fog Hibbert.

The Bracelet of Grood

Norman Moss

Pickering Paperbacks

To Bryn and Sarah

Copyright © 1985 by Norman Moss

First Published in 1985
by Pickering & Inglis,
Marshall Pickering,
3 Beggarwood Lane,
Basingstoke, Hants RG23 7LP,
United Kingdom
A subsidiary of the Zondervan Corporation

ISBN: 0 7208 2367 6

Text set by Brian Robinson, North Marston, Bucks
Printed and bound in Great Britain by
Hazell Watson & Viney Ltd,
Aylesbury, Bucks

Contents

Contents

1: Moonlight's Adventure Begins

Moonlight banked in a graceful curve, and swept in low above the top of the trees. Then with vibrant youth in his wings, soared high till he could see the mountain peaks above the dark line of the forest. At the top of his climb, he went into a backward somersault, wings folded neatly in an instant. It was a stunt he enjoyed, and he had been practising it since dawn.

Now he was in free fall. Arms and legs extended. Wings folded. The ground rushing to meet him. It was dangerous. He knew that. The thrill was to hold on to the very last moment before opening his wings. The wind was making a rushing sound in his ears, the flap of his jerkin was fluttering wildly. His back arched now. He was like a diver about to plunge into the water. But it was the meadow below that was rushing up to meet him. He laughed for sheer excitement. At the very last moment he triumphantly spread his wings, and swept within an inch of the dew that glistened on the grasses.

Extending his toes, he raised spray from the tips of the grasses. It was like sparkling drops of silver in the light of the sun. His neat elfin slippers turned from pale green to dark as they were saturated with water. But the swish of the wet grasses was delightful as they bent beneath his feet.

He soared up again and glided back in the direction of the forest. It was great to be a young elf flying in the beams of morning sunshine. Turning somersaults, darting more swiftly than the swallows. Climbing higher than the skylarks. Only to plummet down in an exhilarating fall. He couldn't resist glancing at the spread beauty of his own wings. Finer than the most delicate silk, the light shone through them, and they displayed all the colours of the rainbow. He knew that even among elves he was something special, and he was proud of the many coloured beauty of those splendid wings.

But even the joys of flight couldn't satisfy him in the end. He was hungry for adventure, longing for the spice of greater danger. Lured by what his parents had forbidden.

All morning long the thought had been in his mind, even as he had hovered on the up currents of air. He had been giving himself a dare. Now he knew his mind was made up. He knew of the cruelty of the Goblins. He had heard the legends told by starlight among the Standing Stones, the tales of the old warfare long ago. . . . There were also more recent stories, whispered among his friends at Merlin's Academy where he was studying for his Diploma in Applied Magic. Stories to make the blood run chill. . . . But then he had made up one or two of those stories himself, and although he knew Goblins existed they seemed rather unreal. Tales to scare an elf child, but not such a one as himself.

"What could a Goblin do to me?" he said to himself. "I would be far too quick and clever for them."

So with his heart beating a little faster than usual, and delightful tingles of anticipation running up and down his spine, he glided down to the foot of the great gnarled trees of the dark forest.

When he landed in the woods, there was nothing to make him afraid. The trees were like those in his own enchanted woodland. The mushrooms were of familiar sizes and shapes and colours. He felt a little disappointed to come so far without an adventure. Eventually he followed a path which led down into the darkness of the forest. Once or twice he glanced over his shoulder, thinking that someone was following, but the path behind him was empty. At last the path led out onto a patch of rough moorland beyond the wood. The ground was purple with heather, which towered high above Moonlight's head, higher than any mushroom.

He was just about to spread his wings to fly back to the enchanted wood, when he came upon a sight which caused him to stiffen with horror. At first he could not believe his eyes, but a second glance convinced him beyond a shadow of doubt. His short life in the enchanted wood had really been very sheltered, and he was not prepared for the horrors of Goblin Land. Hanging from one of the sharp spikes of a gorse bush, was the pathetic skeleton of an elf. Moonlight went closer to see. He could only hope that the elf had been dead when he was hung there, but it looked as though the spike had been driven right through him! Moonlight stood rooted to the spot with horror. He was aghast at the dreadful sight. What cruel fiend could have been guilty of such a monstrous deed? A horrible fascination seized him and he stared wide-eyed wondering what age the elf had been when it had been caught. He was so engrossed with these thoughts that he never noticed the heather stir behind him, nor the two long bony hands which stealthily reached out to grab him by the neck from behind. . . .

The first Moonlight knew of his danger was when he felt himself in a vice-like grip. It was as if a lobster had seized his neck in its claw. Moonlight could not scream, nor even breathe. His wings buzzed helplessly for a moment, and then hung limply as he collapsed into a merciful unconsciousness.

When he opened his eyes, he was lying helplessly tied hand and foot, looking up to a small circle of daylight, which was fast disappearing above him. He

was in the bottom of a large bucket, and a rope was tied to its handle. The rope led upwards to a big pulley at the top of the mineshaft, and then ran down again past the edge of the bucket in which Moonlight lay, and out of sight below. Moonlight guessed that there must be another bucket which went up as his bucket went down. Sitting on the edge of his bucket, and leering down at him with a fiendish grin was the ugliest, crook-backed, old Goblin that you could possibly imagine. Half of his teeth were missing, and his eyes were huge because of always peering in the dark. Lying across the Goblin's knees were what Moonlight thought at first was a delicate net. The next moment with returning consciousness came a sharp scratching pain in his back, and with a sudden terror he knew what the net was on the Goblin's knees.

"What have you done to my wings?" Moonlight screamed.

"You won't need wings where you are going," sneered the Goblin. "They will make a dainty shawl for my daughter."

Moonlight lay, a bundle of misery in the bottom of the bucket, while the pulley creaked and the bucket swayed its way deeper and deeper down the shaft into the depths of the mine. Eventually the bucket came to rest with a jolt. The faces of several other Goblins peered in over the edge of the bucket. One was holding a hurricane lantern, the lamplight striking up upon their faces seemed to make their grotesque features even more fiendish than ever, if that was possible. Moonlight shut his eyes tightly. His last moment had surely come, he thought. The Goblin who had seized him in the daylight far away, now picked him up bodily and flung him over his bony shoulders like a sack of coal. So the wretched Moonlight was carried through long corridors and down rusting iron ladders deep into the lowest galleries of the pit.

Several days dragged by. Not that Moonlight could tell whether it was day or night in the dark gloom of those deep caverns.

Moonlight did not expect to live long in that darkness, but he was a tough little elf. The pain in his back soon eased, but there was no sign of new wings growing. He toiled with the others in the chain gang, pulling the heavy trucks along, each with its dusty load of stones and boulders.

The Goblins said that they were mining for gold and jewels, but Moonlight never saw any. Indeed part of the stupidity of the Goblins is that they will work for years, breaking up mountains, looking for jewels where none are to be found. Yet the Goblins will go on working and working until in the end the whole colony dies out, and all that is left is a patch of flints or shale.

The others in the chain gang were as miserable as himself. Some were Goblins who had borrowed from other Goblins and got into debt. Some had taken to eating orange passion sweet. This is poison to gnomes and elves, but although it may bring a Goblin to the chain gang, it rarely kills him. Then there were elves in the chain gang as well. But they were mostly very old, and their senses had gone through being too long away from their own world. When work stopped they would sit without talking, staring out into the dark, or else they would lie on their sides muttering meaninglessly.

There were other creatures in the chain gang also. Moonlight did not know the names of them all. Some had many arms and legs. Others had no faces at all. Sometimes a fight would break out. Perhaps because one of the chain gang had tried to eat another. But most of the time they were too tired and too frightened of the Goblins with their stone truncheons, to give much trouble.

Fortunately Moonlight had a small appetite even for an elf. He had dined well on a blackberry the day he left home. That would keep him going for some days yet. Others in the chain gang were less fortunate. The Goblins did give them some food, just so that they could keep working, but Moonlight felt that it would be a long time before he could fancy dead wood lice, and that sort of food. If only there had been more light in the pit he might have managed fairly well. Of course Moonlight could give out light himself, but if he did so, he would soon run out of power altogether, unless he could recharge himself in the sunlight or from a bright lantern.

Although things were already bad, there was worse to come. There is something more terrible than living in the dark, and that is to have darkness within you. It happened like this. The Goblin miners had a pet named Grood. It would be hard to describe what he looked like. He was long, and had a great many legs. It was easy for him to live in the mine. He fitted into the long narrow tunnels comfortably, and if he could not see the way he gave out a pale blue phosphorescent light.

He was always gentle in his speech, and popular both with the Goblins and with the chain gang, although had the weaker ones paused to wonder what Grood had to eat they might not have liked him so much! Grood found Moonlight one evening when the elf was sitting on a rock with his face in his hands.

"They were very cruel to take your wings!" he said tenderly.

The elf gave a little sob, he was not used to kindness.

"I think that I can help you," said Grood. "It is not so bad down here you know . . . there are ways to be comfortable . . . I quite enjoy myself. You must not fight the darkness. That is the secret. You live with Goblins, well then become a Goblin, think like a Goblin . . . you will be surprised how much it helps."

"How can I possibly think like a Goblin?" asked the elf.

"Hold my paw," said Grood.

Cautiously, Moonlight took hold of it.

"Now feel my arm."

Encircling his arm was a bracelet. Now Moonlight did not know this, but each of Grood's many arms and legs had a bracelet like this. Unless Grood could get rid of them all he was condemned to staying in the mine. Such was the spell upon him. The only way in which he could improve his lot was to get rid of all the bracelets by giving them to others.

"That" he declared "is the bracelet of Grood.

Because you are a nice little elf, and I have taken a fancy to you, I will give you a bracelet."

"What will happen to me if I wear your bracelet?" Moonlight asked him.

"You will understand things differently . . . you will like the dark. The Goblins will count you as one of themselves. You see how popular I am with them, it will begin to be like that for you too."

"Will they really like me that much?" asked Moonlight.

"Well," said Grood hastily, "of course it will take time, but as the spell of the bracelet begins to work on you things will get better and better. The Goblins will like you, and when they find their jewels in the mine, you shall have a share."

"If the bracelet is so good, why give it to me?" Moonlight wanted to know.

"Oh," replied Grood easily, "I have plenty more."

This was undeniable. Moonlight could not count the number of Grood's legs, and on nearly all of them there was a bracelet.

"Hold my paw tightly," ordered Grood. "The bracelet will slide on to your hand."

Something inside Moonlight warned him not to trust Grood, but he was so weary of life in the mine that he felt that nothing could be worse than what he knew at the moment.

"Now," went on Grood, "breathe in deeply."

Moonlight did as he was told, and as he breathed

in, the bracelet slipped down over Grood's paw and on to Moonlight's arm, as though drawn by an invisible thread.

Moonlight felt the cold ring of steel tighten about his wrist, and as it did so, the darkness of Grood came into his heart.

2: The New Prisoner

In a sense, what Grood had said was true. Things were different now. The Goblins seeing the bracelet began to be much more friendly towards him. Unfortunately, however, they were not very friendly even towards one another. In fact they were given to quarrelling and to moodiness. So their friendship was a rather uncertain thing.

Then again, the darkness of the mine no longer troubled Moonlight. It now seemed soft and velvety to him. He no longer desired to charge himself in sunlight. Instead even the light of the Goblins' hurricane lanterns seemed to glare and dazzle, and hurt his eyes. He no longer thought of escape. Indeed it was hard to remember what the world above him had been like. Time passed, but he hardly noticed it passing. He was living in a daze.

So what Grood had said was partly true. But it did not mean that he was happy. Instead there was always a misery in his heart. He felt that the darkness all around him had penetrated his heart and his every mood.

Sometimes he found himself thinking cruel Goblin things, and yet at the same time despising himself for doing so. He would pinch and kick and torment the others in the chain gang. They all feared him. Even those who were bigger than he was himself. Wearing the bracelet of Grood seemed to give him a kind of frenzied strength.

Then he noticed that he was beginning to get hungry. Not with a gentle elfin hunger for luscious blackberries, but with a horrid Goblin hunger. In dark corners he would stuff horrible things into his mouth. He would fall asleep at night dreaming of eating others in the chain gang. He would work out plans in his mind for setting upon them when no one was around, and feasting himself. He told himself that when the bracelet had made him a little stronger, and he was getting stronger all the time, he would seize one of the weaker Goblins in a corner of the mine, strangle him and then devour him joint by joint.

The next moment he gave a shudder, and wondered to himself that such a hideous and revolting Goblin thought could have ever entered his elfin mind. He realised that more and more he was becoming an elf with the thoughts and feelings of a Goblin.

Once, when he was brooding on what had happened to him, he tore the bracelet of Grood from his arm. How it hurt! His wrist was scraped and sore by the time that he got it off.

How thankful he felt to be rid of the bracelet. That night he slept better than any night since he had entered the mine. He thought that the Goblins would be angry with him . . . but it was worth it to be rid of the bracelet.

He woke the next morning feeling as moody as ever. He opened his eyes, and stared at his wrist in horror. The bracelet had slipped back on to his wrist. Frenziedly he tore at it, breaking his finger nails, but it was now too small to slip over his hand. Try as he would he could not be rid of it.

So the time dragged wearily by. Day followed day. Night followed night. But day and night were all the same in the deep gloomy caverns and galleries of the mine.

One day, the Goblins dragged in a new prisoner. He was another elf, and about the same size as Moonlight. In the old days Moonlight would have felt sorry for him, remembering how he had felt when he first came to the mine.

He would also have been glad to have someone to talk to. Now, with the bracelet of Grood upon his wrist, his only thought was how to make the other elf more unhappy, and to "score off" him in some way.

The newcomer lay bruised from the rough handling he had received from the Goblins. His wings had been torn off. One ear was bleeding, they had pulled it so hard. His face bore the marks of their fists, and scratches from their fingernails.

Moonlight stood by the elf listening to him as he panted and groaned trying to get his breath back. Moonlight, his lip curling unsympathetically, looked down at the prostrate figure. He stood with his hands in his elfin pockets for a moment or two, and then gave the new elf a sharp kick in the small of his back.

"No time to laze around," he said scornfully. "Moaning won't do you any good . . . there's work to be done."

Something in the way in which the new elf came to his feet made Moonlight flinch back. He was no bigger than Moonlight, but there was an air about him. Moonlight realised at once that this elf was far stronger and more formidable than he had thought. Looking at the set of his jaw, Moonlight decided not to have a fight with this elf after all, if he could help it.

However, despite the kick he had received, the new elf seemed to be friendly. He looked at Moonlight with a wry grin, and a twinkle in his eyes. Then he held out his hand.

"My name is Dawnstar," he said. "What is yours?"

Moonlight hesitated. For some reason he felt afraid and ashamed. He did not like to give his real name. Perhaps it was the bracelet which made him reply "You can call me Dusky. . . "

Dawnstar gave Moonlight a searching glance. It

was almost as if he knew the elf's real name. Then he lowered his gaze.

"All right . . . Dusky. Pleased to meet you. I hope we shall be friends."

The Goblins worked Dawnstar unmercifully. They sensed his strength, and wanted to weaken him before he became a danger to them. But Dawnstar never protested or complained.

Moonlight, wearing the bracelet of Grood had special privileges. In fact there was very little for him to do. He had time to stand and watch Dawnstar working. It never occurred to him to give Dawnstar any help. He would put his hands in his pockets and whistle, or sit on a rock tossing up stones in the air, and catching them on the back of his hand. Yet despite himself, he found himself admiring the strength and the patience of the other.

"I wonder whether he has spent his magic yet?" Moonlight thought to himself. He knew that some elves have amazing powers of magic. He had been top of his class at the Academy, but he had heard of previous students who had been brilliant to the point of genius. Could this elf be of that kind? Was he, he wondered, an elf of the High Table? It would explain a great deal if that were so. Yet even a High Table elf would not have shown the patience that Dawnstar did.

Dawnstar never showed any fear of the Goblins. Yet they could hurt him badly, and often did so. One in particular would often use his stone truncheon on

Dawnstar. More than once he left the elf bruised and breathless on the ground. On several occasions Moonlight hung around while these beatings were going on, hoping that Dawnstar would lose his temper, and suddenly unleash all the magic of the High Table. But he never did.

Another very interesting thing was the attitude of Grood. The creature was absolutely petrified with fear of Dawnstar. Grood always avoided him. He would never willingly come into the same part of the mine as the elf. If they did happen to meet, Grood's whole body would tremble with fear, and he would slink away as fast as his multitudinous legs would carry him.

"Why doesn't Grood talk to you?" Moonlight asked Dawnstar one day.

"Well Dusky, we did talk together once . . ." replied Dawnstar.

"What did he say to you?"

"He said that if I would wear one of his bracelets, he would help me to be King of the whole mine, and that he would show me where the treasure of Grood is hidden."

"What did you say to that?"

"I told him who my Father is," replied Dawnstar.

"Who is your Father then?"

"I will tell you one day . . ."

"Tell me now!"

"You are not ready yet."

23

This conversation left Moonlight feeling rather uncomfortable. He did not understand what Dawnstar meant. He told himself that he did not care either. But that was not true. He did care. He cared a great deal. In fact the more he thought about it the more it seemed to matter. Curiosity was mingled with jealousy. He thought about Grood. Why had Grood offered Dawnstar so much more than he had offered Moonlight? This kind of dark thinking was easy for him now he wore Grood's bracelet.

"I am just as important as Dawnstar," he told himself. "What's so special about Dawnstar . . . why shouldn't I be King of the mine?"

The more he thought about it, the more angry and jealous he became. He began to avoid Dawnstar. For several days he would not speak to him at all. And all the time he brooded darkly. Eventually he decided to speak to Grood. He could not find him at first. He tried several tunnels only coming to a dead end. But at the bottom of another he sensed his presence, and spoke into the darkness.

"Why did you tell Dawnstar that he could be King of the whole mine?"

"I beg your pardon, dear elf!" said Grood in a voice of honeyed sweetness.

"I do beg your pardon most humbly . . . I have just been having a little nap . . . such a pleasant dream too . . . however, of course I am always so very, very delighted when you bring your little problems to me . . . now, what was it that you said?" He emitted a faint blue glow as he spoke, and in its light Moonlight ought to have been able to discern a cunning glint in his eye. The elf was far too worked up to notice that, however.

"What makes Dawnstar so important!" he demanded angrily.

At the mention of Dawnstar's name, a quiver seemed to run the whole long length of Grood's body.

"My dear sweet elf! . . . ah, I see how it is, your feelings are hurt . . . very natural of course. It is such a pity that we cannot all be . . . well . . . what shall I say?"

Of course, Grood's heavy attempt at tactfulness only made Moonlight angrier than ever—which was precisely what Grood had intended.

"I ought to be King of the mine!" he shouted.

"Hush . . . Hush . . ." Grood soothed him anxiously. "Of course I like you much better than . . . the other elf." He seemed to dislike mentioning Dawnstar's name.

"Would you really like to be King?" he went on.

Moonlight nodded. The thought of ruling over the Goblins and the chain gang appealed to the darkness within him.

"I wouldn't mind . . ."

"And have the treasure of Grood too?" whispered Grood eagerly.

Moonlight nodded again a second time.

"Well then . . ." said Grood, "come with me . . ." He backed his long length deeper into the darkness of the tunnel. Moonlight followed him until they came to Grood's lair.

"He isn't near is he?" whispered Grood nervously.

"No, of course not!" Moonlight soothed him.

"Come very close then . . . I want to whisper in your ear."

Moonlight put his pointed ear close to Grood's dribbling mouth. The creature's breath smelt of decay, but Moonlight no longer cared about that.

"Kill him then . . ."

"Kill who?"

"You know . . ."

"No I don't. Kill who?"

"The . . . the elf."

Moonlight knew well enough what Grood meant, but he did not want to understand.

"Which elf?"

"The one who . . . who . . . who calls himself D . . . D . . ." Grood shivered, he just could not get the word out.

"Why should I kill him?"

"If you kill him you will prove yourself fit to be King of the mine, and I will help you and give you the treasure of Grood."

Moonlight considered the idea. Part of him did not wish to take Dawnstar's life. Part of him was jealous and dark and with the bracelet on his wrist, he felt that he could do it.

"I must do it when he is asleep," said Moonlight. He licked his lips. "He is too strong for me when he is awake."

"Look then!" Grood pointed with a front leg into a corner of his lair. Lying on the floor was a bright silver dagger. "I have kept it for this day . . . take it, it is sharp and deadly . . . it will slide between his ribs swiftly . . . his blood will flow." Grood was dribbling so badly that saliva was running down on to the floor. It was a sickening sight, but the Goblin

27

mind had control in Moonlight now, and he almost found Grood attractive.

Moonlight stooped and picked up the dagger. He put it to his lips and kissed it. "Pretty silver dagger— you shall win me a crown, you shall bring me a treasure, I shall be rich, I shall rule."

"Ahem . . ." Grood cleared his throat. "It would be well dear elf . . . of course, it is not for me to hasten your departure . . . but perhaps, if while he still sleeps?"

"Yes, I will do it . . . I will go now."

Stealthily Moonlight crept back along the tunnel. The knife in his hand made him feel strong and brave. The bracelet on his wrist poured its darkness into him, and his thoughts were of cruelty, and greed, and hatred, and pride. He pictured the very place on Dawnstar's body where he would plunge in the knife. . . .

3: Dawnstar's Gift

Dawnstar stirred in his sleep. Moonlight held his breath. He raised his arm. Suddenly Dawnstar opened his eyes, and looked straight up past the blade of the dagger at Moonlight's face. "Why do you hate me, Moonlight?" he asked.

Moonlight gasped. "How do you know my name. I told you that I am called Dusky."

"No—your name is Moonlight . . . I have always known that . . . I have known you a long while . . . why do you hate me?"

"I don't really hate you," said Moonlight. "But Grood says that if I kill you he will give me his treasure."

"Well then, you will have to kill me of course," said Dawnstar sadly.

Moonlight raised his hand again. Dawnstar did not shut his eyes, he continued to gaze steadily up into Moonlight's face. A struggle was going on in Moonlight's heart. Suddenly he flung the dagger away from him into the darkness.

"No!" he cried. "You are too good . . . I cannot do it!"

"Come nearer to me then," said Dawnstar. "Take my hand."

They sat in the darkness and Dawnstar talked. He talked of the light and of flowers, of running water, of bird song. He talked of the things in the world above the mine.

He talked on gently and lovingly until at last Moonlight began to cry, which was something he had never done since he first wore the bracelet of Grood.

"If only I had my wings again! How I would fly from this horrible place!"

"I cannot give you your wings," said Dawnstar, "but there is something I will give you if you would like it."

He moved his hand, and on it Moonlight saw a beautiful golden ring, with a lustrous ruby set in the centre of it. The ruby glowed a deep rich wine colour.

"I never knew that you had a ring!" Moonlight exclaimed.

"You can only see it through tears," said Dawnstar. "This is my Father's royal ruby. It has power. If you want to have it, you may take it."

Moonlight tried to protest but Dawnstar cut him short.

"There is not very much time now," he said. "You must prise out the ruby with a dagger."

Obediently Moonlight picked up the dagger again.

"Bend back the golden clasps which hold the ruby in place," commanded Dawnstar.

"But it will hurt the ring and spoil it," objected Moonlight.

"Nevertheless that is what you must do . . . you will understand better later."

The sharp point of the dagger slipped beneath the golden clasps of the ring. In a few moments it was free from the setting.

"Hold it tightly and never lose it," said Dawnstar. "It will help you."

"But your ring is ruined!" cried Moonlight. It was true. The ring robbed of its ruby was ugly—like a socket without an eye.

Dawnstar glanced at it.

"I like it better that way. If you guard my ruby till I ask for it again, I will be well content."

At that very moment there came the noise of a gang of Goblins coming down the tunnel towards them. They could tell that Grood was with the Goblins, for they could hear his voice.

"Moonlight has killed him I tell you."

"Let's make sure that he has done a good job."

"Quickly," whispered Moonlight. "If they find you they will kill you. They are all afraid of you, and when Goblins fear they kill. You run away. I will stay here and make up some story or other. You can escape."

For a moment a frown clouded Dawnstar's face. "I

do not need your lies," he said scornfully. Then he stood up and stepping forward called to the approaching gang of Goblins, "I am here, what do you want?"

Moonlight could see the cruel features of the Goblins as they huddled together in the light of the lantern which one of them was carrying. They were swinging their rough stone truncheons. In the darkness behind them Moonlight could hear the whispering of Grood.

"The little traitor has failed us. You must finish him off yourselves. I know who he is. He will destroy us all. Club him. Kick him. Beat him. Crush him. Attack together. He cannot defeat you all. Seize him. Seize him. Tear him. Smash him. Quickly. Quickly . . ."

The sinister Goblins advanced upon Dawnstar. The lantern cast their grotesque shadows upon the roof and walls of the cavern.

Terror seized Moonlight. He fled further back into the darkness of the tunnel.

Then above the whisperings of Grood and the fierce growlings of the Goblins, Moonlight heard a merry laugh. It was the tinkling of a waterfall tumbling among the stones. It was the bursting of spring leaves. It was birdsong and sunlight. It was the chuckle of a baby. It was the song of the lark. It was all that lives. It was all that sparkles. It was all that shines . . . it was the laughter of Dawnstar.

"Cudgels, bludgeons,
Dungeons, truncheons,
   What are they?
   I know no fear,
Prisons dark
And caverns winding.
Now my spell upon you binding.
   Feel the brightness
   of my spear!"

Suddenly a blaze of brightest sunlight split the gloom of the mine. The roof above the Goblins' heads seemed to cave in. With a terrible rushing and thundering the rocks came crashing down. Moonlight fled along the tunnel choking for breath in the thick clouds of debris.

Suddenly, the light went as quickly as it had come.

Behind him all was silence . . . as the silence of a tomb.

4: The Giant, the Squid and the Pink Spider

After a while, the dust began to settle. No more rocks fell. Cautiously, Moonlight retraced his steps. The tunnel was blocked off with a fall of rocks. If there were any Goblins alive on the other side they could not get at him. Exploring in the other direction, he found that the tunnel seemed to lead on. He groped his way forward and turning a bend he saw ahead of him a glimmer of light. Eagerly he hurried towards it and found himself in a new cave. A ray of bright sunlight slanted down from a hole high above in the roof of the cave.

If only there was some way of reaching it! But although he explored every inch of the walls there was no way to climb. The rock face was smooth. How Moonlight longed for his wings. He would have spread them, and in a moment he could have soared upwards to the light and to freedom and joy.

Nevertheless, the light itself was good. So very good. He stood in the centre of it, and allowed the sunlight to soak into his being. In this way he was recharging, because as you know, sunlight gives energy to elves. It was refreshing, life giving. Better than a night's rest. Better than a good meal. Better than a cool drink. Eventually he felt satisfied. He knew that he had absorbed all the light that he could. Feeling stronger and happier than he had felt since entering the mine, he decided that the only thing to do was to explore on further.

Now the tunnel went down sharply. The floor was covered with loose stones, and he began to fear that the whole floor might begin to slip and slide away. He went very cautiously and after a difficult descent he found himself on level ground. The next moment he gave a cry, for his feet were plunged into icy cold water.

Reluctantly, he decided that he must use a little of the light he had absorbed. For a second he flashed out a fairy glow at full power. The light showed a dark expanse of water. Far in the distance he could see the other shore, but the water looked very deep. He sat down in the darkness to think.

He could swim across of course. But the water looked dark and threatening. He wondered what might lurk beneath its surface. Also he would not be able to shine his light once he got in the water, and he feared that in the total darkness he might lose his sense of direction and wander in circles. Should he go back? He remembered the rock fall. Even if he could shift the boulders he would only be back with the horrid Goblins again. He would have to go on. He thought of Dawnstar, and wondered what had happened to him. Had he been killed in the rock fall? He almost wished he himself had been killed. It would be better than the miserable darkness and coldness and loneliness. How he wished Dawnstar had come with him! Then he remembered the ruby. He fished it out of his pocket and held it in his hand.

"Oh dear!" he sighed to himself. "If only I knew what to do!"

Then he heard Dawnstar's voice. It did not so much strike his ears as speak in his mind, but the words were clear.

"Why not ask?"

"What shall I do?" he said aloud, and the voice replied, "Look for the stepping stones."

There was nothing for it but to shine the light again. At first he thought that the voice had misled him, but when he looked closer he saw that there were indeed stepping stones. Perhaps the waters of the lake had risen, because the stones were just submerged.

Walking on the stones he would be able to shine his light and see where he was going. He stepped on to the first stone and began to look for the second one. It was not too far away. He splashed on to it. The water about his ankles was bitterly cold. It must have been almost at freezing point. His ankles ached like toothache with the cold, and his feet were numb. He leaped from stone to stone, and had counted forty-six stones before he saw that he was almost in reach of the shore. Forty-seven . . . forty-eight . . . forty-nine . . . fifty. There were fifty-two stones in all. Just as he was about to step from the safety of stone fifty-two on to the shore, he suddenly felt his ankle seized from behind. Looking down he saw with terror that it had been caught in the curl of a long tentacle.

Something hideous was gripping his ankle. A dark greyish green on top, it was covered on its yellow underside with orange suckers. He kicked frantically, but the pull was too strong for him. In a second he had overbalanced and with a splash he tumbled into the ice cold water. His light began to fade. Desperately he clung on to the stepping stone with his arms. The ruby, which he had been clutching in his hand, fell into the water. He could see it lying in clear water on the sandy bottom of the lake. The tentacle was pulling harder and harder. Something enormous lay in the depths back there behind him!

He cried out for help, knowing that it was useless. He was quite alone. Yet he could not help but shriek in terror. At the same time, whilst struggling to keep a hold on the rock with one hand, he reached down for the ruby with the other. He was sure that his last moment had come, but if so then he wanted to die with Dawnstar's ruby in his hand. He blazed elf light extravagantly. He must see!

But as he cried for help a strange thing happened. The ruby seemed to be melting in the water. The waters around it turned to a large blood coloured stain, and then beneath the waters a shape began to form. It grew larger and larger, and then, ruby red in colour, a giant raised himself out of the water like a swimmer surfacing from a dive. He brushed back his crimson hair with a scarlet hand and shook drips of water from his cheeks and forehead. One gigantic hand reached out to clutch Moonlight, and a terrible tug-of-war began.

Moonlight felt that he was being torn in two! The tentacle would not let go of his ankle, and the giant would not let go of his hand. The next moment the giant's other hand had the tentacle in its grip, and Moonlight was dragged ashore, and with him came the tentacle. But it was only the tip so far. The giant dug his heels into the sand and leaning back pulled with might and main. Suddenly, like the uprooting of a tree, a gigantic squid came to the surface. Moonlight saw that he would have been no more than a tiny nibble for the creature's enormous beak. The squid was still holding on beneath the water. The giant's muscles rippled and bulged. Moonlight dropped clear as the tentacle suddenly lost its strength.

Then he heard the two speaking, although again

the words were in his mind rather than in his ears.

"He is my lawful prey!" shrieked the squid.

"Never!" the giant replied sternly.

"But he has the bracelet of Grood on his wrist. He is an escaped captive from the Goblin mine. He has escaped them, but he shall not escape me!"

"It is true that he has the bracelet of Grood, but he has the ransom ruby too. He is a captive no more. The stone is the sign of his reprieve . . ."

"Give him back to me, or I will take him by force!"

"He is reprieved. I shall deliver him."

Then a fearsome struggle began again. The giant had enormous strength, but the ground upon which he stood was fine and powdery sand. It was difficult for him to keep his footing. His heels drove furrows through the sand. The squid was also immensely strong, and had the advantage of tentacles beneath the surface holding on to rocks, though some of its tentacles were already maimed by the first tremendous tug which had brought the squid up from the depths.

So the struggle went on. Yet the giant never looked anxious. Even at a point in the battle when the tentacles coiled about him like boa constrictors, he still remained calm.

The end came suddenly. With a terrible cry, the squid, its tentacles trailing limply, was pulled right up on to the shore. The giant raised his foot and placed it upon the evil creature of the deep. As he did so, it suddenly shrivelled away, and out from under the foot of the giant fled a centipede shape with a drooling mouth and bracelets on many of its legs. It was tiny. Not much larger than Moonlight himself. No more than an insect compared to the size of the giant. Moonlight recognised the creature at once. It was Grood. In a moment Grood had found a crevice and wriggled away into it.

The giant, stooping, picked up Moonlight in his hand as if he was a piece of thistledown. "You are safe now . . ." he said. "I must leave you."

"Are you a genie?" asked Moonlight.

The giant laughed. It was a pleasing sound like the booming of waves upon the shore.

"No, no, little one. You summon a genie with magic, but there is no power to summon me. My name you may not know, and perhaps you will not see me again . . . but cling to the ruby . . . from the ruby some help will always come . . . . although not always the help you would wish. Sometimes the ruby is strongest when it seems most weak."

"Where am I to go?" asked Moonlight.

"Why, follow the scarlet thread of course . . ." said the giant.

Stooping low, he set Moonlight gently down upon the soft sand and the next moment he was gone, and the ruby lay at Moonlight's feet. As he stooped to pick it up, Moonlight saw a red thread lying on the sand. It was no thicker than the strand of a cobweb, but it led on across the sand. Holding the ruby tightly, Moonlight plodded on.

At the further wall of the cave he found a crack. The thread led inside. Squeezing in, Moonlight followed it. He found himself in another tunnel, but it seemed to him that there was some light ahead.

Then, for the first time he felt a breath of wind. Eagerly, he hurried forward. He saw ahead of him a gap. He ran on and the next minute found himself dancing in the sunshine and the open air. He was free of the terrible Goblin mine!

*

He did not recognise this side of the mountain. He guessed that he was many miles from his own enchanted woods. He found some luscious blackberries and replenished himself. Then he lay down and slept in the warm sunlight. He woke just as the sun was setting. He had hoped that when it was dark he might see the light of some fairies, or gnomes, or elves. They might be able to tell him the way. But there was no sign of any magic light at all. Only his own glow, and he switched that off to save his reserves. He decided that it would be best to spend the night where he was. He was afraid that in the darkness he would not be able to follow the thread. So he lay, wide awake through the night. He was quite happy, for he made himself a cosy nest of dried moss, and tucked himself up in it. He lay on his back with his hands behind his head, watching the moon riding high through wisps of fleecy cloud. The night was brilliant with stars and beyond them the sky was a deep purple.

When dawn came he stood up, brushed his clothes down with his hands, put the ruby carefully in his pocket and looked round for the thread. It lay, the faintest of pink lines over the dew-spangled grass. It was not at all easy to see the thread in the light of the dawn, but he followed it carefully. Once, when he stopped to look round at the scenery he thought that he had lost it altogether, but after an anxious search he found it again and hurried on. Then he saw ahead of him a boundary fence and some trees. An elf shorn of his wings travels very slowly and perhaps it was not really as far as it seemed to him, but by the time he reached the shadow of the great trees, the sun was high in the sky.

The thread led him through the woodlands until at last he came to the edge of the wood and saw across lawns to a great house standing on a hill in the distance.

Moonlight did not like the look of that house at all. He was a creature of the wild enchanted forests and had been taught to beware of all houses—for in them, so his mother had warned him, dwelt HUMANS, with fly swats, and all sorts of human magic.

This house was dark and sinister. Even in the light of midday it was gaunt. Its towers looked as though they were the haunt of bats. Its lower windows were protected with iron bars, as though there might be dungeons behind them. The house had an untidy, neglected appearance. The drive up to the front door had potholes in it, and what flowers there were seemed straggly and in need of water. The more Moonlight looked at this house, the less he fancied the idea of going near it. Yet the thread led across the lawns towards the door.

While Moonlight sheltered in the protection of the woods, fearing to cross the exposed lawns, he heard a clopping and a scrunching sound. A very old carriage appeared on the drive leading up to the house. It was drawn by a sleepy old grey horse. The carriage was black. Seated on the driver's bench, and dressed in an old fashioned and rather dingy coachman's uniform, was a large toad. He held the reins carefully, but seemed content to let the horse amble along at its own speed.

As the carriage passed near where Moonlight was hiding, he could see the passenger inside. The sight was not encouraging. It was a creature of human shape, but the face was covered with wool so that it looked something like a goat or a sheep. Horn-rimmed spectacles were perched on the creature's nose and it seemed to be reading a book.

The carriage stopped at the door of the house. The toad coachman climbed down, opened the door of the carriage and let out the ungainly bespectacled figure of its Master. The ill-assorted pair shuffled up the steps of the mansion and when the door had opened, they went inside. The horse lowered its head and began to nibble at a tuft of grass growing up through the gravel of the drive.

Moonlight pondered the situation. It was true that the thread led towards the door of the mansion. But what if it was a trick? He did not like the look of things at all. Perhaps there were two threads, and he had followed the wrong one! Or perhaps he was not supposed to follow the thread in the sunlight. Maybe it had only been there to guide him out of the cave.

The house did not seem to be anything to do with him. It was too big. Toads and sheepmen were not for him. He was an elf. He loved the sunlight. He loved birdsong, blackberries, running water, and being outdoors. He had escaped from a chain gang and he did not want to enter a prison.

Just then he heard the sound of the tinkling of tiny bells. Looking up towards a bluebell he saw the first fairy he had seen since his capture . . . and fairies and elves are near kin.

"Cooey," she cried. She was dressed in a pretty blue dress.

"What is your name?" called Moonlight.

"Tansy," she replied.

Eagerly Moonlight climbed up to sit beside her.

"Whatever happened to your wings?" she cried.

Moonlight avoided the question. "I'll tell you later," he said.

"What is this place?" he gestured towards the house.

"Oh," she said. "It is a terrible place . . . there is nothing happy there. It is called 'Slocumbe House'. They do say that there are torture chambers, but all I know is that it is sleepy and dusty and dreary. Very few people go into it. Even fewer come out! But what are you doing here? I thought that I was the only fairy in these parts!"

"And I thought I was the only elf!"

They laughed together. Moonlight realised how good it was to have company again. Suddenly he knew that he had been very lonely.

"Let's play 'Hide 'n Seek'," said Tansy.

"Oh no," said Moonlight. "I want to look at you, that is all. Let's keep together."

"Silly," laughed Tansy, wrinkling her nose. "You can look at me any time . . . I want to have a game!"

"All right then," said Moonlight.

"Count up to ten," she said.

Moonlight counted and heard her call in the distance, "Cooey."

Eagerly he ran after her. He searched this way and that, and eventually found her curled up inside an empty snail shell. Then it was his turn to hide. He found a good hiding place deep in the hollow of an old oak tree. She was a little cross by the time she found him.

"You shouldn't choose such hard places!"

So the game went on, and while the toad coachman of Slocumbe House led the horse to the stable, and put the carriage under shelter for the night, Moonlight and Tansy played a game which led them deeper and deeper into the forest. Moonlight was covering his eyes and counting when he heard the fairy shriek. He ran down a path and found himself near an old pond partly overgrown with ferns. A broken drainpipe was near, and across the mouth of it was an enormous web. The fairy was trapped in the sticky web. It held her clothing and her long golden hair. Frantically she struggled, twisting this way and that, and as she did so, she called anxiously for help.

"Moonlight . . . oh help me, Moonlight . . . oh Moonlight."

He ran towards her. Suddenly from out of a hole at the side of the pipe four great bony legs reached out and grasped the meshes of the net.

Moonlight grabbed a stick and ran towards her. He brought the twig down with a smack across the bony legs. As he did so, he stumbled and fell into the net himself. With a rush the great goggle-eyed spider with his pale pink body was upon them. Struggle as they might he began to spin, and they found themselves cocooned in two white envelopes of web.

Then he spoke, and his words were brief and horrible.

Tapping Moonlight on the head with a cold bony finger he said, "Breakfast." Then digging another bony finger into the fairy's middle he said, "Lunch."

Then he edged his fat pink body back into his hole. He drew his legs into the hole out of sight and lay still. For a while they could see his eyes staring greedily at them, but then the eyes closed in sleep. Nevertheless, the delicate tips of his legs still held the lines of the web, as an angler might drowse with a fishing line.

"Oh Moonlight!" sobbed the fairy. "It's all my fault!"

Moonlight shook his head, "I should never have left the scarlet thread."

"What do you mean?"

Moonlight told her his story while the spider drowsed on.

"Will the crimson giant rescue us?" she asked eagerly. Moonlight shook his head.

"I have disobeyed . . . I don't think that he will."

A tear rolled down Tansy's cheek.

"I wish the spider would eat us now . . . this

waiting is so terrible."

Moonlight struggled desperately in his cocoon, but he was quite helpless.

Just then, a large stone in the bank of the pond began to move. It fell with a plop into the water, revealing a hole behind it. From out of the burrow appeared a familiar drooling mouth and the first of many pairs of legs

"Grood!" cried Moonlight.

Grood was at his most affable. "I see that you are a bit tied up at the moment," he said.

"Please Grood, do get us out of this!"

"Certainly, certainly ... it will give me the greatest pleasure ... of course for a little consideration ..."

"What do you mean?"

"Give me the ruby," said Grood. "If you will promise to give me the ruby, then I will set both of you free."

"Please Moonlight!" begged Tansy. "What use is the ruby if we are eaten. Do what he says."

Moonlight shook his head desperately. "Dawnstar gave it to me and told me to keep it. You don't know Grood as I do. He is treacherous and evil!

"Charming!" exclaimed Grood. "Don't spare my feelings ... you can see how it is, my dear. This elf prefers his Dawnstar to you!"

"Set us free!" pleaded Tansy. "I will do anything you want!"

Grood considered. "Will you wear one of my bracelets?"

"Yes, yes, anything," cried Tansy.

"You mustn't," whispered Moonlight with desperation in his voice.

Grood shuffled towards Tansy, and bit at the cocoon around her tiny feet. He held up a paw, and a bracelet slipped up from his paw on to her ankle.

Moonlight groaned. He saw the darkness enter Tansy's face just as long ago in the dark mine the darkness of Grood had entered his own heart.

"Well at least keep your bargain!" he cried. "Set her free as you promised!"

"All in good time . . ." said Grood. "First give me the ruby."

"Never!"

"I hear that the spider is a slow eater!" said Grood pleasantly.

"No!"

"I hate you Moonlight!" cried Tansy. "Why won't you do as he says, then he will set us free!"

"I would rather that we were both eaten by the spider than go back with Grood," said Moonlight stubbornly.

"Please, please, dear Grood, set me free. Never mind about him . . ."

Whether Grood would have freed Tansy or not cannot be said, because the whisperings and strugglings woke the spider and he came out on to

his web.

"Ah . . . Grood," he said consideringly. "At your old games again I see!"

Grood smiled ingratiatingly. "I see you have had a good catch," he said.

"If you behave yourself, you may have the bones," promised the spider. "But go away now, you are trespassing you know. I shall call the ogre if you don't go."

Evidently this threat meant much to Grood. All his legs trembled, and murmuring apologies he backed into the tunnel and disappeared.

Tansy flamed with temper. "You horrid creature

. . . why didn't you give that nice Grood the ruby—all our hope is gone . . . it's all your fault."

Moonlight said nothing. He knew that it was really Tansy who had got caught at first, but he could not feel cross with her, because he remembered what it was like to wear the bracelet of Grood before Dawnstar gave him the ruby.

For a while they hung silent in their cocoons, each with their own thoughts. The spider returned to his lair.

5: Slocumbe House

The night was dark. An owl hooted in the distance. In his heart, Moonlight called out to Dawnstar, but nothing happened. Then he saw a lantern coming along the path. It travelled jerkily, and the yellow light cast weird shadows. Moonlight thought of the spider's words about the ogre, and his blood ran cold. What further horrors could this night hold? As the lantern drew near, it was clear that its owner was carefully searching the woods as he came. Eventually Moonlight decided that not even an ogre could be worse than being eaten by a spider.

"Help!" he cried.

The lantern came near, and as it did so Moonlight saw that it was being carried by the toad coachman of Slocumbe House.

"Ah, there you are," said the toad. He had a croaking voice, but it was not unpleasant, and he sounded greatly relieved. Reaching up a webbed hand, he brushed the cobwebs down. With deft fingers, he loosened the captives' bonds. From deep in the safety of the hole, they could hear the spider grumbling and complaining.

"Night's work . . . new web . . . interference . . . lawful pursuits . . . game preserves . . ." Those were some of the words they could hear. Others were indistinguishable, and some were distinctly rude. The spider was not at all pleased!

However, the spider was no match for the toad, and he did not dare to leave the safety of his lair.

"Follow me," said the toad. Moonlight and Tansy did as they were told. Fear kept Tansy close to Moonlight.

"Will he take us to the ogre?"

"Where are you taking us?" Moonlight plucked up courage to ask.

"To friends," was all that the toad would say.

He led them up the long drive to the house. There were some lights in the windows, and it looked more attractive in the dark.

The door swung open to reveal a large hall, with a log fire burning merrily in the grate.

"Come into the library," said the toad.

The sheepfaced man was sitting in a large padded leather armchair by another fire. A mellow oil lamp with a glass chimney was on the table at his elbow. He looked down at the tiny bedraggled pair before him. Seen close up, his face was gentle, kindly, wise and friendly. "You should have followed the thread to my door," he said to Moonlight.

The elf hung his head.

"The bracelet will bring you much sorrow," he said sadly to Tansy.

Tansy flamed into a temper at once. "What business is it of yours?" she flared back at him.

"There, there," soothed the sheepfaced man. "You are tired and hungry, and you need sleep."

He rang a bell at his elbow, and the toad appeared again.

"Refreshment, Poddle, refreshment for our guests."

"Of course, Mr Carer."

"Is that your name?" asked Moonlight.

Mr Carer nodded and smiled. "Come and warm up by the fire," he said.

Soon Poddle was back with a wooden tray loaded with the things that fairies and elves like to eat.

"Poddle is an excellent cook," said Mr Carer, while they enjoyed the food and hot drink. "I do not know what I should do without him!"

"Is there anyone else here?"

"No, just the two of us. We have been here a long while, too long perhaps. But we have a few guests from time to time. Not as many as we used to have, I am afraid."

When they had finished their meal, Poddle returned, and Mr Carer said "Now Poddle, show our guests to their rooms."

Tansy had a room in the East Wing. It was plainly furnished, but Poddle had been busy with the

warming pan. The linen on the four-poster bed was warm and welcoming.

Before Tansy went to bed she tried hard to pull Grood's bracelet off her ankle. But no amount of effort would do it. She only made her leg raw and sore, and in the end she climbed sadly into bed and lay quietly sobbing until merciful sleep came and with it oblivion.

Moonlight was humming quietly to himself as he got ready for bed. He took the ruby out of his pocket and put it under his pillow. Before he went to bed he stood looking out of the window and spoke softly into the night, "I am sorry. I ought to have followed the thread." There was no reply . . . but he felt his words had been heard.

A bright ray of sunshine striking through the casement woke Moonlight from a deep slumber. He lay enjoying the luxury of a warm bed. He could hardly believe that his time in the mine had not been a bad dream. He glanced round the room looking at the furnishings which he had not been able to see the night before. There was a dark coloured chest of drawers with big round wooden handles. A wash stand with a marble top stood in one corner. On it was a bowl and a jug of water. The wardrobe was of mahogany and had a full length mirror. By the window was a low wooden chest with a padded cushion on it. The pattern was a sort of patchwork of bright colours. The room did not look as though its owners had much money to spare, but on the other hand it was nice and comfortable in an old fashioned sort of way. There was a knock at the door, and Poddle entered with a breakfast tray. "I hope you slept well?"

"As deeply as Merlin, thank you Poddle . . . I feel strong again . . . if only I had my wings . . ." he sighed.

"Never mind Sir . . . when you come to your journey's end, you will find your wings again, I am sure! Enjoy your breakfast Sir, it will give you strength for the journey."

There was a steaming bowl of honey dew and a

delicious fruit salad. A glass of fresh milk. Soft white bread with a golden curl of butter. Moonlight sat up in bed and feasted himself until he could eat no more.

Tansy also woke to a happier day. Poddle had thoughtfully heated a quantity of water for her to bathe in. She came back into the bedroom after her bath to find a silver tray with a dainty breakfast. Poddle had gone to the trouble of picking a little bouquet of wild flowers. He had put them in a tiny vase on the tray.

"Why are you so kind?" she asked.

Poddle shuffled his feet and looked a little awkward.

"We just want you to be happy, that's all . . ."

They stayed in Slocumbe House for all that day. They explored the rooms and wandered in the grounds. They found that the house was much more pleasant inside than it seemed when viewed from outside.

"We used to have a lot more people to help," explained Poddle apologetically. "I do what I can, but I am afraid it isn't all that it should be."

When they were alone Tansy told Moonlight that the house needed what she called a "woman's touch". Since Moonlight had no idea what that might be he did not contradict her.

There was a lovely picture gallery with huge oil paintings on the walls in heavy gilt frames. Most of them were pictures of humans and the world of men and women. So of course Tansy and Moonlight could not make much of it. There was a picture of a man and a woman and a tree, with a snake curled round it. Moonlight said that something about the snake's eyes reminded him of Grood, but Tansy told him not to be silly. There was a picture of a man sitting in a den of lions, yet none of the lions was eating him.

Right at the end of the gallery was a picture of a beautiful city more lovely than anything they had ever seen. The streets were bright and shining, and the gates were a lustrous white. The picture was signed at the bottom by the artist, John Bunyan. "I wonder who he was? I wish I knew the stories of these pictures . . ." said Tansy.

Then they wandered into the library which was full of leather-covered books. These were too heavy for them to lift down from the shelves. So they went on and found a whole gallery full of old suits of armour and other weapons. Moonlight enjoyed looking at it very much, although of course it was all far too big for him.

That night they sat by the firelight in the study whilst Mr Carer—his spectacles perched on the end of his nose—read stories to them out of a great leatherbound book with huge brass clasps. Poddle sat in a chair in the lamplight whittling away at a shepherd's crook. He had a big pocket knife and was a wonderful carver. He was shaping a thistle flower on the end of the curl of the crook. When the story was finished they all sat staring into the fire. The silence was cosy. Sometimes a coal would shift with a dry scraping sound. The flames leaped and danced. Moonlight could see all sorts of pictures in the glowing coals—castles—streets—grottoes.

Suddenly Tansy gave a deep sigh.

"Your stories are lovely, Mr Carer . . . if only . . ."

"If only what, my dear?"

"If only I did not have this cruel bracelet on my ankle."

Mr Carer's deep gentle eyes gazed down at her, then he looked towards Moonlight.

Moonlight said, "I know just how you feel. I used to feel just the same, but it has been easier for me since I had Dawnstar's ruby."

"I wonder whether Dawnstar escaped?" said Tansy.

Mr Carer smiled.

"Of course he escaped . . . why, he was here this morning."

Moonlight leaped to his feet eagerly.

"Where is he? I want to see him!"

"Sit down again," said Mr Carer gently, "you cannot see him now, but you will see him one day."

A terrible thought was beginning to form in Moonlight's mind. A cold shiver ran down his spine.

He felt miserable and wretched, but the silence seemed to challenge him. He swallowed hard, and trying to sound pleased at the idea, he spoke again.

"Mr Carer?"

"Yes Moonlight?"

"Mr Carer, if I were to give Tansy my ruby, would she feel as happy as I feel now?"

"But if you did that Moonlight, you would not have the ruby any more!"

Moonlight swallowed again.

"But Tansy would be all right!"

"Ask her then, Moonlight!"

His mind made up, Moonlight brought out his ruby and looked at it for the last time as it lay on the palm of his hand.

"Tansy, take it . . . I would rather that you were happy than be happy myself!"

To his surprise Tansy shook her head. "No Moonlight," she said gently. "I cannot have your ruby—I don't even think that it would work for me . . . though if it would I wouldn't take it from you. Dawnstar meant you to have it, not me."

Then she sighed again and added, "How I wish that I could meet Dawnstar, and that he would give me a ruby of my own."

Suddenly Mr Carer gave a delighted chuckle. "Ah, how I have waited to hear those words!" he said. "Fetch the box, Poddle."

Poddle put down his work and left the room. He

returned with a small mahogany chest with brass bindings and hinges. Mr Carer produced a key and put it in the lock. From inside the box he took out a tiny jewel case covered with bright green leather.

"When Dawnstar called, he gave me this for you, but he said that I must wait till you asked for it."

"What is it?" she cried eagerly.

"Open it and see!"

She pressed the tiny catch, and the jewel case sprang open with a click. Inside, nestling on the green satin, was a tiny golden ring, and set within the clasp a small ruby.

"Oh, please may I have it?"

"Of course."

With a cry of joy, she slipped it on to her finger and began to dance with delight as only a fairy can do. The room flashed and glowed as she sped from place to place like a spark of fire. The air was filled with the tinkling of silver bells and the rippling of fairy laughter. Unless you have seen a fairy dance, you cannot imagine what it was like. Humans see something like it on the 5th of November when they run through the black night whirling sparklers. The difference is that when fairies dance they sparkle with all the colours of the rainbow, and each spark has its own music.

"Now young lady," said Poddle at length, "you will make my old master's head ache with your excitement."

Tansy was all contrition at once. "Oh please forgive me, dear Mr Carer!" she cried, coming to rest on the carpet at his feet. "I have never been quite so happy in all my life before!"

"There, there," said Mr Carer. "I love to see you happy, only remember that there are dangers ahead."

He looked towards Moonlight with one of his gentle smiles, "And now, Moonlight, Dawnstar gave me a present for you, but he said that first you must offer to share your ruby—so I can give you your present now."

This time, Poddle returned with a rusty tin box. Moonlight tried not to look disappointed, but it did not look as though such a dowdy box could hold anything worth having. He tried to open the box. At first he could not lift the lid at all, but with Poddle's help he managed to get the box open. It came undone with a squeak.

Then Moonlight gave a delighted cry, and leaned forward eagerly. In the bottom of the box lay a sword in a scabbard. It was just the size to fit

Moonlight, and there was a belt to go round his waist.

"The scabbard is not very pretty," said Tansy.

"It is for use," said Mr Carer. "Draw the sword, Moonlight."

Once again at first Moonlight could not do it. The sword seemed stiff in the scabbard.

"It will come with practice," said Mr Carer.

The next moment Moonlight drew the sword. There was a sharp crackle like a tiny explosion, and the sword leapt from the scabbard. Tansy flung up her hands to cover her eyes. It was so bright—it was not a blade of steel—it was a blade of living fire.

"Only use it against Dawnstar's enemies," said Mr Carer.

6: Follow the Stream

The next day, Tansy and Moonlight set out on their travels again. Mr Carer came down to show them the way. "You do not follow the scarlet thread any more," he said. "The thread only leads to my door. From now on you must keep by the stream." He showed them a little pool. It was brimful with clear water. From the pool there trickled a tiny stream. It flowed over the stones, and down a waterfall. "Follow this stream. Whatever you do, don't leave it. But first, before you go, taste the water. Then if you are in any doubt you will know which is the true stream by the taste of the water." They stooped, and held their cupped hands under the trickle of the waterfall. The water was fresh and pure. It was icy cold. When they had sipped the water, they said goodbye to Mr Carer, and made ready to go.

Just then, Poddle came down from the house. He had two sticks, and on the end of each stick there was a bundle of food wrapped up in bright coloured handkerchiefs.

"Here you are," he croaked cheerfully. "Food for

the journey. It would not last me long, but you two have such small appetites that it should keep you going for days."

"Thank you, dear Poddle!" said Tansy.

"I wish you could come with us!" said Moonlight.

Mr Carer smiled, and shook his head. "We shall see you again, never fear, but we cannot travel with you—you see there are the others who will come this way."

"Goodbye then," they cried.

Mr Carer and Poddle stood and waved as the two of them set off together, following the stream.

"Will they be all right?" asked Poddle anxiously.

Mr Carer smiled. "Yes . . . I know they will be . . . they will be all right in the end."

"You know Tansy, I wonder whether I ought to leave you behind . . ."

They were sitting on a dry stone with the water of the stream rushing and gurgling past them. Tansy was dangling her feet in the icy water, enjoying it as it tickled her toes.

"Don't you want me to come with you?" she said with a dimple.

"Of course I do . . . you know that . . . it is only that . . . well, it may be dangerous and there is no need for you to go."

"Oh yes there is," she said. "You want your wings, but I want to thank Dawnstar for my ring, and where you find your wings, I think somehow that Dawnstar will be there too."

All that afternoon they walked by the stream. The sky was blue and the meadows white and gold with daisies and buttercups. The stream flowed deeper and fuller now. It began to be too wide to cross.

"I wonder which bank of the river we ought to be on?" Moonlight wondered.

"We must make up our minds . . . because it will soon be too deep to change."

"Perhaps it doesn't matter which side we walk so long as we follow the stream."

By the time they camped for the night the stream had become a deep flowing river. They slept under the shelter of an overhanging boulder, lulled to sleep by the steady rush and swirl of the water.

Next day the sunrise woke them. The ripples of the river were sparkling golden where the rays of the sun struck across them. Although the ground was soaked with dew, they hurried on their way, determined that next evening would find them near their journey's end. By the middle of the morning they came to a bend in the river and found rising in the distance before them the gaunt shape of a water mill. The whole river flowed in under a huge iron grating, and disappeared into a murky blackness beyond. The mill itself had a high square tower at one end with a pointed roof. The windows were small and covered with iron bars. The red bricks were blackened with age, but nevertheless the place seemed to have been kept in good repair.

"What now?" asked Moonlight.

"Mr Carer said that we were to follow the river—but what happens when the river goes inside a grating? I wonder what is on the other side—it may be a dangerous weir or something."

They sat down where they could see without being seen to consider the problem.

"Moonlight . . ." said Tansy apologetically.

"Yes?"

"I hate to mention it, but I do still have my

wings—could you bear to be left here while I go and reconnoitre—or do you think that that would be breaking our promise to Mr Carer?"

Moonlight considered. "I am sure that it is all right to be careful, and I will stay here. You go—only *do* take care—remember the spider!"

Tansy shuddered. "I am not likely to forget."

With that she spread her wings. Moonlight felt a little envious of her powers of flight, but he realised that if she was patient enough to put up with his slow walking, he ought to be grateful not envious. He ate a little food and drank from the stream and just when he was beginning to get anxious Tansy came sweeping back with a low graceful dive.

"You fly well," he admitted.

She coloured and bobbed a curtsey. "Thank you . . . I am out of practice really."

"What did you see?" he asked.

"Well," she said, "I am glad that I went—I do not like the look of it at all . . . the front is quite different from the back. . . . It is very smart—a paved court-yard and fountains, and plate glass doors at the entrance.

"There was a big sign outside it said FLOWING WATERS CO. LTD.—BOTTLERS AND DISTILLERS. While I watched, two great tankers arrived, and also several vans with crates of bottles. There are loading bays. It is a big factory, with lots of people coming and going . . ."

"I don't like humans!" said Moonlight. "I am afraid of them."

"These are not exactly humans . . ." said Tansy. "They are rather . . ." she hesitated and then added, "sort of wolfish, really."

"What do you mean?"

"Well, they have bodies like Mr Carer's, but their faces look villainous and their jaws are long, and they have too many teeth and their tongues are long, and hang out . . . where are you going Moonlight?"

"Back to Mr Carer!"

"But wait . . . we can't go back—he said go on, we must follow the water."

"We have followed the water—we cannot go any further—iron gratings and wolf men! I'm scared!"

"Well, at least wait . . . I haven't finished yet!"

"What else did you see?"

"It was a funny thing, but I don't know where the water goes to. The water runs in there, but it doesn't come out."

"What about the fountains?"

"I don't think that they used the same kind of water at all . . . it looked to me as if they were run by a pump using the same water again and again."

"Well, what shall we do?"

"I think that we must go in—after all, Mr Carer said follow the water."

"How can we go in?"

"I could fly."

"You are not going without me—we must go together . . . wait a minute . . . you see that big leaf up there?"

"Yes."

"Could you fly up and break it off?"

"I think so."

"Well, you, see we can float on it."

Tansy did as Moonlight had suggested. The big leaf curled like a canoe, and sitting upon it they launched out into the current, and floated swiftly down towards the iron grating.

7: Terror Beyond the Mill Wheel

After the sunshine, it was so dark that Moonlight instinctively gave out his brightest blue glow. It was just as well, because they were nearly caught in the paddles of the great mill wheel. It was turning slowly in the water. Each great blade scythed down with the water dripping from it in heavy drops. The wheel creaked as it turned, and the water roared past in a cataract. Above their heads, huge iron cogs meshed their teeth, and axles squeaked. The din in the enclosed place was terrific. Mercifully, Moonlight was able to grab a projecting iron spike before they were swept under the wheel.

"Quickly," he cried. "This way!"

The wall above the spike had enough projections for them to be able to leave their makeshift canoe, and climb high above the mill race. Soon they were on a level with the cogs, and avoiding being caught in the machinery they ventured on past the mill wheel. In the distance before them, they saw a small grating, and clambering towards it over slimy wet brickwork they peered through.

Beyond them lay a great lake. On the right hand side of it were a number of iron wheels and other machinery which seemed to control sluices. They realised that the mill was on high ground. The country beyond the mill looked arid and desolate. Trees were straggly and what grass there was seemed brown and scorched.

"Why," gasped Moonlight, "they have cut off all the water."

"There is another grating over there," Tansy whispered.

Cautiously they crept over towards their left. This gave them a view over the courtyard which Tansy had seen before. They could hear the rush and swish of the jets of the fountains. From below them came the hum of machinery which drove the centrifugal pumps. As they peered down into the sunlit court-yard, they heard the sound of a lorry arriving.

The lorry was an old-fashioned one with a high driver's cab and a round iron tank at the back. The driver pulled to a halt and clambered down stiffly from his cab. Two wolf men came out on to the paving stones to meet him. Tansy and Moonlight could hear their conversation.

"Please let me have some water free," pleaded the man. "My crops are withering in this sun—how can I pay you unless I sell my harvest."

"No more credit for you," snarled one of the wolf men.

74

"Promises, promises . . . they are no good. We cannot build our college of aquatics on promises . . . you must sell your lorry and carry the water in buckets!"

The man fell on his knees and lifted up his hands imploringly.

"I cannot do that—my crops will die!"

Just then an older wolf man came out of the building. His hair was long and silver grey. It was almost the colour of sheep's wool.

"Now, now," he said in a gentle voice.

"You must not be hard on this poor man . . . Here my good fellow, I will help you . . . sign this paper. It says that you will give us your land when you die. Sign this and you can have all the water you like."

"Thank you Sir, thank you!" cried the man kissing the old wolf man's paw-like hand.

"There, there," said the wolf man.

"Go and fill your lorry with water from the pipeline."

"It's wicked," Tansy hissed indignantly. "The water is free. It is Mr Carer's water, and they are making them pay for it."

"Shh," whispered Moonlight, "they will hear you." He drew her back from the grating. Nearby was a circular staircase with iron rungs, winding down to the floor below. Cautiously they crept down the staircase, and found themselves in a large store room. There were vats, and huge glass jars.

One wall had wooden racks with rows of empty glass bottles. In another section bottles filled with liquid lay in rows carefully protected with straw. At the far end of the room was shelving with row upon row of chemicals. It was like a laboratory. Tansy flew up to one of the shelves and began to read out the labels.

"Self-help additive. Crystallised hypocrisy. Good-deedseed (dried). Emulsified whitewash. Conscience palliative. Diluted truth (thinners). Smooth syrup."

"Try the next shelf," called Moonlight.

Tansy flew down. "Polish," she read. Then she flitted to the next bottle. "Extract of culture. Educational digest powder. Preserved habits. Custom powder."

Then she came to a section labelled MINERALS.

"Gold dust. Refined oils. Silver nuggets. Hardening salts."

"Be careful with those jars at the side there, they are acids," Moonlight warned her.

"Plain truth—highly corrosive. Spiced secrets. Antagony—bitters. Spirits of spite."

Near the door was a section full of beautiful cut-glass decanters. Again Tansy called out the labels to Moonlight. "Elixir of luxury. Beauty lotion—highly volatile. Smarmoil. Wheelgrease. Love potion—handle with care. Distilled greed—deadly poison."

Moonlight tiptoed over to a hatchway in the floor. Peering down he could see complicated machinery below. A never-ending belt carried bottles jogging on their way past a machine which filled each bottle in turn with liquid. The machinery was noisy and clattering. Some bottles, very much like those on the shelves in the laboratory, were connected by transparent plastic tubes to the same machine, so that a few drops of the concentrated fluid was being added to each bottle full of water.

"If the people are only getting drink out of those bottles they are all being slowly poisoned," Moonlight thought to himself.

"What do we do now?" asked Tansy alighting on the floor beside him.

"I don't know that there is much that we can do . . . we are so small!"

"Well, we had better be on our way then."

Moonlight turned and began to climb back up the circular staircase. It was tiring work for him, for the stairs were huge and he had no wings. Coming down had been easier, but this was almost as bad as struggling up the side of a mountain.

Tansy was a little tired of waiting. She flew up on to a table and began to look at her reflection in a small mirror. She patted her hair, and twitched uneasily at her gown. This travelling rough was hard on one's appearance. While she was occupied at the mirror, the door behind her opened. She did not hear it because of the clanking of the machinery in the work room below. A bespectacled wolf-man entered. He gave a gasp of astonishment and then began to creep up on her from behind.

"Got it!" he clasped his hands triumphantly and cupped Tansy within his grasp like a butterfly. A wolf-boy had followed the man into the room.

"Get that jar!" the wolf-man ordered.

Very cautiously he stuffed poor Tansy into a large jar, and then pressed a rubber bung into the broad neck of the jar. Tansy lay crumpled in a heap on the floor of her glass prison.

The wolf-boy gave an excited gasp. "It's a fairy!"
The wolf-man squinted at him through his heavy

spectacles. "A what?"

"A fairy!"

"Don't be so stupid you silly lout—there are no such things as fairies!"

"What is it then?" asked the boy, none too politely.

"We shall see in a minute . . . some kind of moth or butterfly . . . fetch me that specimen board, and my magnifying glass."

The boy went to a large white cupboard in the corner and returned with a large wooden board covered with white paper. On this board a number of dead butterflies were transfixed. Each had a long pin stuck through the middle of its body.

"Now get my tweezers out of that drawer . . . and some glue . . . and that box of long pins . . . mmmm! . . . very interesting . . . fairies indeed!"

Grunting scornfully to himself, the wolf-man arranged the board on the bench and put the tweezers in place. He selected a long pin from the box.

"Now when I take it out of the jar, hold the wings open and I will stick the pin through the middle of its body."

"Will it hurt?" asked the wolf-boy.

"I don't know," said the man indifferently. "Be thankful you are not a butterfly . . ."

Moonlight was climbing as fast as he could down the steps again. The wolf-man and the boy were too engrossed in their task to notice him. He leapt the last stair, and ran across the floor till he was hiding under the shelter of the table. The wolf-man's trouser leg was near him. He drew his sword.

"Now boy . . . open the bottle . . . shake the butterfly on to the board. I have the pin ready . . ."

It was no time for half measures. Moonlight drove the bright flame of his sword into the wolf-man's ankle.

"Ouch!" The wolf-man was hopping up and down in agony. "I have been stung! First butterflies, now bees. Take my arm, boy . . . get me to the sick bay . . . I am in agony . . . it burns like fire."

The pair hurried out of the room. Moonlight clambered up the tubular leg of the stool like a boy shinning up a telegraph pole. With an effort he swung himself up on to the seat, and then on to the table.

The rubber bung was still in the jar. Frantically he tried to prize it out, but he could not even reach it properly.

Tansy was crumpled in a pathetic heap. She was on the point of suffocation. What *was* he to do? He decided that desperate measures were called for. He put his back against the jar, and pushed with all his might. Suddenly the jar began to slip. It skidded to the edge of the table, and smashed to the floor. Tansy lay stunned amid the shattered fragments. Moonlights slid down the tubular leg, and ran to her. He shook her by the shoulder, frantically calling her name. With the fresh air, she began to revive. He was able to half drag, half carry her under the shelter of a nearby cupboard. Underneath the cupboard it was like a dark cave. He longed to make a dash for it, but Tansy was not yet strong enough to fly, and in any case, he knew it would be too risky to try and climb the staircase. So the rest of that day, they lay in terror under the cupboard. The wolf-man returned with a bandage round his ankle. He cursed the boy for breaking the jar, and sent him for a dustpan and brush. Both of them seemed to assume

that the "butterfly" had recovered and flown away.

Towards evening the two of them went off to tea. The wolf-man was still limping. Later the machinery stopped, and all was still, except for the distant creaking and splashing of the waterwheel, and the rumble of the iron cogs. It began to get dark.

"We will give it another hour," whispered Moonlight, "then we can make a run for it."

Tansy was much better now, and impatient to go. Moonlight still insisted that they should wait. The laboratory was in almost total darkness when they finally crept out and began to climb back up the steps again. Tansy wanted to try and carry Moonlight, but he would have none of it.

"You must not strain your wings," he said. "Especially after the shock you have had."

So Tansy flitted from step to step, while Moonlight struggled up again. Just as they reached the top step, the door opened, and a torch beam shot out in the darkness. The light played on to the table, and then began to search the shelves systematically. As the light caught the mirror on the table, it reflected back enough illumination for Moonlight to see that it was the wolf-boy.

"I am sure it was a fairy," they heard him whisper to himself. "She must be here somewhere . . ."

The light began to play over the floor and found its way towards the circular staircase.

"Quickly," whispered Moonlight. He leaped

towards the top step and hauled himself on to the flat surface.

Then the light caught them in its beam. The wolf-boy let out an excited gasp, and came rushing towards the steps. In an instant they reached the darkness of the upper loft, from which they had entered earlier in the day. The boy was swinging his torch this way and that; it threw shadows from the long beams which ran up from the floor to support the roof. There was silence except for the boy's panting breath, and the creak and splash of the waterwheel.

"Fly through the grating," hissed Moonlight. "I will join you on the edge of the reservoir by those sluice gates which we saw."

"What about you?"

"I have an idea! But fly quickly—you are safe enough. He will not be able to catch you, and you will take his attention from me!"

"All right! Here we go!"

Tansy spread her wings, and sped towards the grating. The boy caught her in the beam of his torch and ran eagerly towards her, but it was too late. In a moment she was in the air and speeding low across the water towards the sluice gates. Taking advantage of the distraction, Moonlight ran towards the revolving mill wheel. He flung himself upon the great wet blade of the revolving wheel. As the blade swept down, he flung himself into a dive out into the foaming water of the mill race. Holding his breath, he was swept along in the fast rushing torrent and out into the still water of the reservoir.

8: The Proffitt Bird

Moonlight was a good swimmer when he had to be. It was a long swim across the reservoir, but he made it. At last, panting and splashing rather, he reached the other side, and clambered up. By the sluice gates he found an anxious Tansy.

"Oh Moonlight," she cried, "are you all right?"

"Yes, fine," he shivered. "Just let me get my breath back. It was as if the water wanted *to carry me.*"

The wolf-boy did not raise an alarm. He did not dare tell the wolf-men that he had seen a fairy. They would only laugh at him. In any case he had lost her. He went back to bed.

Moonlight and Tansy sat on the iron wheel of the sluice gate and looked across the dark reservoir in the pale light of the moon.

"You see what it is?" he told her. "They have cut off the water supply, and taken all the water there is. They bottle it, and add poisons to it, and then they sell it to the people in the valley below us. None of the people are getting pure water any more. They are having to pay for what they get, and it is all spoilt by having things added to it."

"I wish we could do something," said Tansy.

Moonlight looked thoughtfully down over the side of the great dam. "Well we could do something . . . I don't know how much good it would do, but it would be worth trying . . . the only thing is that I don't want to do it unless it is right . . . Wait a minute. He fumbled in his pocket and took out Dawnstar's ruby. He sat looking down at it as it lay in the palm of his hand.

"Tansy . . . do you think that Dawnstar would want the people to have to pay for the water?"

"No."

"Neither do I . . . I am sure that we must do something . . . did you do magic at school?"

Tansy shook her head. "Not much . . . I used to have a magic set at home, I was given it for a present, but the experiments were rather dull."

"Well, I can do a bit . . . not difficult stuff like shape changing . . . but we were doing applied weather when I left . . . I think I might be able to raise a small waterspout . . . only you will have to help me, because I cannot fly any more, and that makes it rather difficult . . . you see we have to make the bobbin."

"The what?"

"The bobbin . . . that's what my Master used to call it anyway."

"I don't think I understand . . ."

"I don't suppose you do, and it is rather difficult to explain . . . but I think it will work all right. At least I hope it will. Here, take these buttons." He tore two of the buttons off his jacket. "Now fly, and drop one in the middle of the reservoir and then fly up about thirty feet and hold the other one. You will be the top of the bobbin. Only take care, because the weather will get rough below you. When the bobbin is spinning well, then fly forward over the dam."

"I wish I knew what you were talking about."

"You will see in a minute . . . only I hope that I remember how to do it, I wasn't paying much attention when we did the experiment at school . . . I never thought it would come in useful."

Tansy flew out over the water as instructed, and Moonlight heard a tiny splash as his button dropped into the water. He moved along the wall to one end of the dam. Tansy soared upwards and hovered over the lake.

"Now for it," he said to himself. He stood on one leg and began to spin round faster and faster. He went round like a humming top till he was no more than a blur of movement, but at each revolution he clapped his hands once. A strange whistling sound came from his lips. Tansy hovered patiently above the lake. At first she thought that nothing was happening. But then as she looked down she saw that round where she had dropped the button the water was beginning to flow in a circle. Moonlight was spinning faster and faster. The noise which had begun upon his lips now had a being of its own. Suddenly Moonlight stopped dead, and flung himself face downward on the ground. Beneath her Tansy saw the waters lashed to a fury. The air beneath was full of spray, storm, violence. The air was filled with a terrifying, weird howling noise. Suddenly, at the moment that Moonlight dropped for cover, the waterspout formed itself. It was a column of water, thirty feet high. It moved as Tansy moved with the button. It was as if the mighty force was tugging at her, like a wild animal. The din was terrific. Tansy hanging on to the button for dear life flew out over the dam, high in the air. As the mighty waterspout hit the sluice gates they were swept away, and the waters swept over the top of the dam. Moonlight felt the masonry of the dam begin to crumble. He raised his head and stared fascinated as the waters roared and crashed in a mighty cataract sweeping all before them. The waterspout was gone, but where it had passed there was a gaping hole in the side of the reservoir. It looked as though some passing giant had kicked a hole in the wall with his foot.

Lights had come on in the mill, and wolf-men were running and shouting. Moonlight took a winding footpath which led down into the valley, and Tansy flew down to join him. By the time

Moonlight and Tansy had reached the valley below, the waters they had freed were already flooding down the river bed.

"Will the wolf-men build the dam again?" asked Tansy.

"Not in our time!" said Moonlight. "Perhaps they will never be able to do it . . . I think it will really depend on whether the people prefer the taste of the real water to that bottled stuff. . . ."

Moonlight and Tansy knelt at a place where the waters flooded swiftly over the pebbles, and refreshed themselves with a wash and a drink. The river gurgled as it flowed.

"I am not sure that it had much to do with my magic really . . ." admitted Moonlight. "It was almost as if those waters had a power of their own, and they just wanted someone to give them a chance to get free."

When they had put a distance between them and the factory, they decided to take a few hours' sleep and to press on their way when they felt wide awake again. The sun was high in the sky when they wakened. They were lying in a grassy green hollow near to the place where they had drunk from the stream.

Moonlight wakened first. He awoke with a start. As he opened his eyes, he saw two bright eyes observing him from a clump of bracken. He went stiff, and lay pretending that he was still asleep. But a cheerful, high-pitched voice cried out, "It's no use pretending . . . I can see you peeping . . . come and have a game!" The bracken waved as the creature, whatever it was, disappeared.

"What was that?" said Tansy rousing herself.

"I don't know," said Moonlight. He was puzzled.

"It was me!" said the voice, and another clump of bracken just above their heads parted to reveal a nose like a rabbit's, with the same two bright eyes.

"Can't catch me," it cried, and disappeared again.

"We don't want to catch you," said Moonlight.

"What was that?" The eyes and nose peeped out from behind a tuft of grass.

"How do you get from place to place so quickly?" asked Tansy, becoming interested despite herself.

"That's the game," explained the creature, "catch me if you can."

Tansy suddenly spread her wings and darted like a kingfisher to settle on the tuft of grass. But the creature was grinning at her from behind a grey rock some distance away.

"Tansy!" cried Moonlight sternly. "Come back at once."

Tansy pouted, but she came. There was something in Moonlight's voice which made her come.

"It's rather fun . . ." she pleaded.

"What did Mr Carer say?"

"He said keep to the stream."

"Exactly. I don't trust that creature."

"What shall we do then?"

"I think that if we don't chase it, it will be all right."

Sure enough the next moment the nose poked out from a small hole not far from where Moonlight was lying.

"You're not much fun," the voice complained. "Where do you come from?"

"We are on a journey," said Moonlight. "We are following the stream."

"Oh."

Suddenly the creature came out into full view. It was the oddest looking thing. It was part feather, and part fur. The feathers were yellow-gold in colour, and the fur was white as snow. Its face was like a rabbit's, and it had very long ears. Its tail was like a big powder puff, but its legs were just like those of a chicken, and it had short wide wings, which it would suddenly flutter and flap as it spoke in its high-pitched voice.

"Look at me!" it cried, flapping its yellow wings, "Aren't I pretty?"

"Not especially," said Moonlight.

"Yes I am," insisted the creature, dancing on one leg, "everybody says so."

"Who is everybody?"

"Why, all the chasers . . . look, here they come!"

The creature pointed into the distance with one

wing. Sure enough, a group of men were steadily beating through the undergrowth in the distance. They looked hot and tired. They had sticks wrapped round with black cloth, and round-shaped black hats. They were working very seriously. Each had a big leather bag.

"What will they do?" asked Tansy.

"Oh," said the creature "they are trying to catch me and my friends. If they can catch me, they will put me in their bag and take me home."

"Will they eat you?"

"Oh no. They will take care of me. They will feed me and pamper me . . . because, you see, I can work magic. Look. The creature flapped its wings sharply, and suddenly a great Christmas tree loaded with gifts appeared where the creature stood. The next moment it had vanished.

"No wonder they want to catch you," exclaimed Tansy.

The creature disappeared and the next moment it peeped out from cover again. "How about you . . . care for a chase?"

"No," said Tansy firmly, "we must keep near the water."

"You're no fun," grumbled the creature. Yet it seemed quite friendly and willing to talk. Perhaps it was so vain that it couldn't resist showing off to them. "You watch . . . I shall have such fun in a minute, when they start to chase me."

"What will happen in the end?"

"Oh, I always get away again . . . I do a bit of magic while they pamper me, and then when I get bored I get away . . . unless I decide to stay, and then I can be horrid."

"Not you," said Tansy, "you are too happy."

"Oh you would be surprised . . . I am not always like this. If people keep me too long, I go broody, and then I start annoying people . . . they get hard and quarrelsome . . . and then when I get tired of them . . . I give them a little nip." The creature put out his tongue and licked his lips. They saw that his tongue was forked like a snake's. "Yes, I give them a little nip . . . and that is the end of them."

Suddenly a shadow fell across the patch of grass. One of the black-hatted man appeared. "Got you!" he shouted, and brought down a butterfly net over the creature. Tansy and Moonlight watched as the man carefully searched the net. They were as sure as the man was that the creature was in the net. But suddenly from some distance away they heard a cackling laugh, and there was the creature flapping his golden wings and dancing round on one pink leg. The man went flying off in pursuit.

"I did that rather well!" crowed the voice, and there he was by their side again.

"What are you?" asked Moonlight.

"I am a PROFFITT," said the creature. "Now watch the fun." It really was a strange sight. The Proffitt suddenly appeared in the middle of the chasers. They let out eager cries and rushed towards it, but it vanished so quickly that several of them banged their heads together and fell over in a heap of waving arms and legs. Then the Proffitt began to run round in circles. Soon a black line of men was running in pursuit. Their faces were scarlet with the effort, and some fell down out of sheer weariness. But the Proffitt bird did not weary. Every now and again it would do its little dance and crow with delight, clapping its funny wings together. The chase grew wilder and faster, far more frantic than the most exciting fox hunt. Yet every now and again the

Proffitt bird would suddenly come back and wink its big eyes and twitch its nose at Tansy before leading them off on another chase.

"Watch me this time!" it said. "I am going to let that fat one catch me . . . I think he is quite the most objectionable of them all . . . so he deserves me. I shall make him thoroughly miserable. I don't think I shall have to nip him even . . . he has made himself so ill chasing me that he won't last more than the night. Then I can have another lovely game tomorrow. Cheerio!"

With these words it disappeared again, and next moment leaped up into the fat man's arms. He clutched hold of it with a gleeful cry, and stuffed it into his leather bag. The other men, looking woebegone crowded round the fat man enviously. Then they packed up their things and went off home with sad tired faces.

"We must be on the move," said Moonlight.

9: The Mist Eeries

By lunch time Tansy and Moonlight had travelled a long way down river. They had eaten all Poddle's food before entering the mill, but there were plenty of blackberries so they were not short of food. They sat on a log by the water and rested for a while. Then they continued walking. As they came round another curve of the river, Tansy gave a delighted cry.

"Look!" she exclaimed. "There's Mr Carer!" The familiar, if rather shabby, figure was sitting on a boulder some way down stream. They hurried towards him, calling his name excitedly. However, as they drew nearer they realised that it was not Mr Carer after all. Nevertheless, the face which turned to look over its shoulder towards them was kind and gentle. There was the same tender expression in the large eyes behind the glasses.

"Hallo. . . ." he said. "You are Moonlight and Tansy . . . I expect . . . my brother told me that you would be coming this way."

"How is dear Mr Carer?" asked Tansy.

"Very well indeed," the other replied. "He heard

that you broke down the dam," he went on, "and he is very pleased with you."

"Those scoundrels were stealing all the water," said Moonlight.

"Yes, I know . . . you did well to avoid the Proffitt bird, we were rather afraid that you might decide to chase him!"

"Oh no!" replied Moonlight. "We understood that we had to follow the water."

"Only as far as here!" said the sheep-faced man. "Now you must go towards the fountain of life. You will be able to see it from that ridge over there."

"Are you quite sure that it is all right to leave the water?" asked Moonlight. His voice sounded worried.

Mr Carer's brother gazed down at him with a mild and benevolent expression.

"Do you think that I would deceive you?" he asked gently.

Moonlight blushed. "Oh no, of course not! It's just that Mr Carer was so very definite that we must keep to the water whatever happened."

The sheep-man smiled. "My brother is an expert on the part of the journey near Slocumbe House, but you have come a long way from there you know, and I am the one who knows most about this part of the journey. If you just run up to the ridge, you will see the fountain of life. All that you have to do then is to keep it in sight, and you will soon be at your journey's end.

"I tell you what," said Tansy, "I will fly up to the ridge, and if I can see the fountain, I will call you."

So Moonlight waited with Mr Carer's brother, until he heard her voice in the distance.

"Come on Moonlight . . . it is beautiful . . . hurry and see."

Moonlight said farewell to the sheep-man and set off along the rough track which led to the ridge.

The fountain of life was indeed a beautiful sight. No words could properly describe it. Although it was far away in the distance, they could see the flashing brilliance, the colours of many jewels. The fountain jet shot many thousands of feet into the air. They could not see the pool from which the fountain leaped skywards, it was too far away. But the sparkling jet was a breathtaking and glorious sight upon the horizon. Eagerly, Moonlight and Tansy began to run towards it.

Once they had crossed the ridge they were out of sight of Mr Carer's brother. He watched anxiously until their figures had completely disappeared.

Then he took off his spectacles, and put them in his pocket. Producing a handkerchief he dabbed at his mouth, which was beginning to dribble at the corners. Then he sighed. He moved his hand and rubbed at the tight bracelet on his wrist.

Already he was shrinking in size, and lengthening

in shape. His mouth was slobbering again, but he did not want to dab at it now. More and more legs were appearing. Had Moonlight been able to look back over the ridge, he would have seen a familiar shape scuttling towards a dark hole in the river bank. Just as he was entering the hole, Grood paused and chuckled to himself.

"My brother Mr Carer . . . Follow the fountain of life . . . How can I trust you? . . . How indeed!" He crawled into the friendly dampness and darkness of his underworld.

"Do wait a minute Tansy!" panted Moonlight. "I am quite out of breath."

They had descended the far side of the ridge, and they were in a great desolate plain. The fountain although it could still be seen in the distance, seemed to be no nearer than before. They walked on.

Several hours later they were still trudging wearily on. Moonlight's legs were aching and his feet were sore. The plain seemed never ending. The landscape monotonous. He had the feeling that he was walking without making any progress at all. Eventually he sank down with a moan.

"Tansy, you can fly. You can go so much more quickly than I can . . . you go and see if you can get help from anybody at the fountain."

Tansy was almost as tired as Moonlight, but her wings were still fresh. She spread them and flew eagerly towards the ever-changing rainbow of colours which shone in the spray of the distant fountain."

Moonlight waited eagerly. It seemed an eternity before he saw a distant speck fluttering towards him. But his heart sank at the thought that she was alone.

When finally she settled beside Moonlight she was so tired that for a moment or two she could not speak.

"Well . . ." he asked eagerly, "what did you find?"

"Oh Moonlight," she said shakily, and there were tears in her eyes. "We have been deceived!"

"What do you mean?"

"We cannot reach the fountain at all . . . I flew until I came to a great cliff. There was a deep rift in the ground. It stretched for miles and miles, there was no going round it. It was so deep that I could not see into the valley at the bottom. I'm not even sure that it had any end at all. It looked as if it went down and down into the middle of the earth. The ground goes on on the other side, but the fountain still looks as far away as ever."

"But didn't you try to fly across?"

"Of course I tried, but there are terrible gusts of wind, and I could not cross at all."

Moonlight stared at her aghast. The same thought had come to them both.

"We have done wrong to leave the river!"

"Yes."

"But surely we could trust Mr Carer's own brother?"

"I am not sure . . . I am not sure of anything any more."

Wearily Moonlight hauled himself to his feet, and Tansy walked dejectedly beside him. Secretly she was thinking that if only she could fly on without him, it would be much easier for her. Moonlight too had bitter thoughts. He felt somehow that Tansy was to blame. If only she had not called him to the top of the ridge. Perhaps they would have quarrelled, but they were too tired even for that. They walked on in unfriendly silence.

The sun was getting low, and they were still not back at the river when Moonlight spoke. "Do you see those tiny wisps of smoke?"

She followed his pointing finger.

"The mist is rising!" she said.

"I hope it isn't going to get foggy," said Moonlight.

They walked on.

The mist was thicker now. It rose in little spouts or columns, swirling about their ankles. It did not seem quite like ordinary mist which swirls in patches across the ground. It was almost like steam emerging from the spouts of hundreds of kettles, but before the water had really come to the boil.

The feel of the mist was chilly and damp. Tansy and Moonlight quickened their pace. Each began to fear that they might get lost in the mist. But although they hurried on, they seemed no nearer the ridge from which they had come. The plain seemed to have no ending.

The mist was rising now. It was up to their chests. The next moment it had blotted out the sun, and was swirling around them. They seemed to be shut in by the fog. They drew closer, and stood together shivering with cold. They did not know which way to go. There was no sound to guide them. They could not see more than a few feet ahead.

"Perhaps it will pass," Moonlight said with more optimism than he felt. "We had better sit down and wait."

Drawing their clothes about them, they sat down. Suddenly Tansy stiffened and pointed.

A shape loomed up for a moment out of the mist, and then disappeared as silently as it had come.

"What was that?"

"I don't know!" Moonlight cupped his hands to his mouth and called out "Hallo ... is there someone about?"

There was no reply ... the mist swirled around them. Even his voice seemed muffled and deadened. When he stopped shouting the silence seemed dead.

"Do you feel as though we are being watched?" Tansy asked nervously.

"Nonsense. How could we be?"

"I don't know ... but it feels like that to me!"

Time passed.

In the end each of them fell off into a weary slumber. Moonlight woke with a shiver. He felt chilled to the bone. He shook Tansy by the shoulder.

"We must not stay here. We shall die in the cold. Besides, it is getting darker than it was . . . we must press on."

"But which way?"

"How do you expect me to know?" he asked irritably. "This way is as good as another."

They set off, groping their way forward.

Suddenly Moonlight drew back with a cry of alarm. A huge grey shape loomed out of the fog. It had a long robe down to the ground, and wore a

hood over its face. Its eyes were two slits in the hood.

Panic stricken, the pair took to their heels and fled.

In absolute silence the grey-hooded ghostlike shape swept down upon them, and then passed over them like a swirling mist. They felt nothing except an ever-greater coldness, but when he had passed by, they were separated from one another in the fog.

"Tansy! Where are you?"

"Here!"

Eagerly he ran towards the sound of her voice, but when she called again she sounded further away.

"Moonlight!"

Now it was truly horrible. Each was lost, and alone in the fog. All that night they wandered over the desolate plain seeking for one another and bewailing their misery. Perhaps the search kept them alive, but they came near to death from the cold.

Coughing miserably, Moonlight wandered on until his feet began to sink in a treacherous bog. Frantically he flung himself down along the ground, and by clutching at the tufts of grass growing in the gravel, he managed to pull himself back to safety. His trousers were soaked in filthy mud. It was too dark to see, but he could feel the slime . . . and smell it too! He lay where he was. He was afraid to move until he could see better. Eventually he either slept or lost consciousness.

When Moonlight awoke it was to find that the fog

was still swirling round him; however there was more light. He guessed that somewhere above his head there must be blue sky and a shining sun, but down below he was in his own damp world of white mist.

Then he saw the hooded figure standing half shrouded in the mist.

"Who are you?" he challenged, gripping his sword.

The voice which replied was like the wind gently stirring amid autumn leaves. It was no more than the faintest whisper.

"I am a Mist Eery."

"Please show me the way out of this fog," pleaded the elf.

"I know nothing but fog," whispered the voice in reply.

"Well I do!" exclaimed the elf stubbornly. "I know blue sky and heather ... bubbling streams, and gorse like a crown of gold and ..."

"The stuff of dreams," scorned the Mist Eery. "There is nothing but fog ... always fog and more fog."

"Take me to Tansy!"

"Another dream," whispered the voice. "You are alone, there is no Tansy, or if there was once, she has gone away long since ..."

Moonlight drew his sword. The flare crackled and flashed as the blade leaped from the scabbard. He brandished it threateningly.

"Stop your lies!"

The Mist Eery laughed gently.

"Come and fight me then."

Moonlight leaped at the hooded figure, lunging with his sword, but the mist seemed to swallow up his opponent.

Moonlight tripped and fell. His sword fell from his fingers. Frantically he seized it again, but now the mist was full of opponents. Hooded figures were all around him. He could hear their whisperings but as he chased one, another and another would crowd in behind him. He ran wildly this way and that. Their voices were all around him. All the time they were whispering questions and uncertainties.

"What makes you think that your sword can hurt us?"

"How do you imagine that you can ever escape from us?"

"This mist goes on forever!"

"There is no way out of it, you know!"

"Unless you jump over the precipice!"

"Or perhaps you may choke to death in the bog!"

"Then of course there is the ogre!"

"Mr Carer is a deceiver—what made you think that you could trust him?"

"There is no fountain of life!"

"Tansy has deserted you!"

"Your sword is quite useless!"

He found that they did not actually try to hurt him. When they came near to him, it was only like the opening of a door into a dank cellar. But they kept on whispering till he hardly knew his own mind at all. He began to half believe what they were saying. Tansy did not care, or she would not have left him in this mist! Perhaps he had imagined Mr Carer and the fountain of life. Even the sword seemed no use at all. In the end he reached such a pitch of despair that he petulantly flung the sword away.

The next minute he regretted what he had done and searched through the mist crawling on his hands and knees while the Mist Eeries mocked at him. After a long search he found the sword, but the blade was gone. Only the hilt remained. He held it in his hand, but no magic revived the blade of flame. Sobbing hopelessly, he flung himself down.

"I wish I had never been born!" he wailed.

"Perhaps you never were," sighed the Mist Eeries, "perhaps you don't exist at all."

Moonlight had now reached such a pitch of uncertainty that even these silly suggestions seemed reasonable to him . . .

10: The Warnings

Tansy also wakened to find herself still alone in the mist. To her, however, the light brought hope. Eagerly she spread her wings and flew upwards. A Mist Eery tried to soak her wings with droplets of dew, but she fought him off, and soon emerged into brilliant sunlight. She hovered looking down upon the mist. It lay a blank white patch upon the plain. Where was Moonlight?

It was the Mist Eeries who unintentionally helped her to find him. So many of them had gathered to enjoy Moonlight's misery that the mist where they crowded together was like a dark grey blot in the white of the fog. The situation did not look very inviting, but she decided to venture.

As soon as she entered the coldness of the Mist Eeries she was encouraged to find that Dawnstar's stone had begun to give out a bright beam of ruby light. It was like wearing a powerful torch upon her finger. The beam pierced the Mist Eeries like a red searchlight. As she shone the light downwards it probed to the spot where Moonlight lay huddled with his arms around his head. As she flew towards him the Mist Eeries fled before the red blaze of light. The white fog remained, however, enclosing them.

"Moonlight!" she called him eagerly.

Listlessly Moonlight raised his head.

"Go away."

"Oh don't be silly, I have come to rescue you."

"Nobody can rescue me!"

"Why ever not?"

"Because I have lost hope, that's why. I don't believe in anything any more."

"Oh Moonlight." She sat down beside him.

"Moonlight. Do you still have Dawnstar's ruby?"

He gave a bitter laugh.

"I have a bit of old red stone," he said.

He put his hand into his pocket and drew out the stone. It was quite true . . . the stone did not look much like a ruby. It was dull and dirty. It looked just the kind of ordinary dusty pebble that you might pick up anywhere in the road.

Even Tansy was a little shaken.

"Are you sure that that is the same stone that Dawnstar gave you?"

"I am not sure of anything I tell you!"

"Oh."

There was a long silence.

Tansy could feel the mist creeping into her. She did not know what to say. Yet she could not bear to leave Moonlight as he was.

"Look at my ring, Moonlight!"

He glanced indifferently at her finger.

"Don't you see how it shines and sparkles? Those creatures hate it!"

"I don't see anything," he said. "It is just an old ring with a bit of red glass in it." As he said these words, the light in the ring went out as suddenly as if someone had blown out a candle.

Tansy felt doubt enter her own mind. "No!" she exclaimed. "It is Dawnstar's ring. He gave it to me."

"But how do you know that?" whispered the Mist Eeries creeping silently towards her and drifting around her. "You only have Mr Carer's word for that. You didn't ever see Dawnstar."

Tansy fixed her eyes upon the ring. "It is Dawnstar's ring," she repeated stubbornly. "I know that it is." As she said the words she deliberately pointed the ring at the nearest Mist Eery. The hooded figure flung up his arms to protect himself, and immediately the red beam flashed forth from the ruby again.

"Look Moonlight! Look!"

But Moonlight would not look.

"Very well then," she cried. "Give me the old stone as you call it! Let me have it, or better still throw it away."

He looked at her doubtfully.

"I don't want to throw it away."

"Why not?"

110

He hesitated. "I don't know!"

"I will throw it away," suggested Tansy pretending to reach towards it.

"No!" He pulled himself up from the ground and seized the stone.

"Why not?"

"Because I like it."

"Why do you like it?"

"Because ... Because it is DAWNSTAR's," he shouted.

As he said these words the stone in his hand suddenly flashed and blazed. A great warmth flooded his heart, and he saw the Mist Eeries for what they were. The heat drove back the mist in all directions.

The hooded figures began to vanish and they found themselves alone on the empty plain.

"How silly I was!" exclaimed Moonlight. "Quickly, let us run back to the river."

Just as they turned to go, however, they found one last Mist Eery lingering by a damp patch on the ground.

"You have beaten us," he moaned in a voice like the wind in the eaves of a cottage. "You have beaten us . . . but the ogre will get you." With that he dissolved into a puff of mist and drifted away.

Back at the river, they knelt upon the bank and drank deeply. For several minutes afterwards they lay resting. Then they heard a voice speaking to them."

"My dear young friends . . . how are you?" A slobbering mouth was peeping out from the ferns.

"Grood!"

"The same, my dear young friends . . . the very same!"

"What do you want?"

"Ahem . . . may I talk to you?"

"Make it snappy!"

"Of course, of course. You won't stab at me with that nasty sword?"

Moonlight, who secretly dreaded that his sword had lost its power forever, said nothing. Grood shuffled a few more of his legs out of the hole.

"You see, my dear young friends, I really feel that I ought to warn you about the ogre."

Despite herself, Tansy felt curious. "The Mist Eery said that there was an ogre!"

"Ah yes . . . those lovable Mist Eeries. They are second cousins of mine you know . . . though I fear they lack my cheerful good nature . . . but I was telling you about the ogre. He lies chained in the river bed some way down from here. He is between you and the fountain of life. You were going to the fountain, were you not? Well I am afraid there is absolutely no way of avoiding the ogre. So you see your journey is a waste of time . . . Rather a pity really . . . If I were you, I would save yourselves trouble and come back with me."

As he spoke, he twitched the feelers beneath his slobbering mouth and at once each of them felt a tug. Moonlight felt it on his arm. Tansy on her leg. The finest of threads, almost invisible and far thinner than the most delicate spider's web, ran from Grood's feelers to the bracelets on their limbs. "You see . . . we have always been very attached to one another," he said in his most dulcet tones.

Instinctively, Moonlight drew his sword. The blade flashed and crackled as it used to do before he met the Mist Eeries.

Grood began to retreat backwards into his hole. "So hasty!" he complained. "I was only warning you, you know . . . no need to go waving that beastly sharp thing about. You will hurt someone one of these days." He disappeared into the darkness, but they had the feeling that he had not gone far, and that his eyes were still furtively gazing at them.

"I never noticed those threads before," said Tansy. "It is horrid to think that we are tied to him."

Moonlight used his sword to try to hack through the thread, but it was so fine that it just clung round the blade without being cut by it.

"Try to snap it."

Moonlight gave a jerk with his hands.

"Ouch!"

The thread cut into his hands like a very sharp wire.

"It's no use!"

"What shall we do?"

"Well, we must go on. That's all. Just keep going."

This time it was Tansy's turn to hesitate. "But what is the use of going if the ogre will get us?"

"I don't believe Grood," said Moonlight stoutly. "I expect he is trying to frighten us. I am going to follow the stream just as Mr Carer told us to do. Come with me!"

Together they set off.

Peering from his hole, Grood watched them disappear into the distance. He twitched with his feelers at the threads. "A little more line yet!" he whispered to himself. "A little more line. Then a little more line. Just a little more . . . then when they are tired, and they see the ogre . . . why, I can pull them back."

11: The Fountain of Life

The stream was beautiful. The water gushed deep and clear. The river was brimming full to the top of the banks. Flowers of blue, and white and yellow and pink grew in profusion in the meadows. Trees, their leaves rich red and gold, hung over the river as if gazing at their own reflections.

Moonlight and Tansy journeyed on and on. Then after some hours, they came to a place where the river entered a deep gorge. The slopes above them were dark with purple heather. Although the sun still shone, the high sweep of the moorlands cast the river into shadow. Picking their way along by the banks of the river, they made slow progress. Then the river turned sharply to the right, and they found themselves hemmed in by towering granite cliffs.

At the far end of the valley the cliffs drew closely together, and for a moment they thought that they were facing a wall of granite into which the river tumbled. Then they realised that they were gazing at a living something, but it took a moment or two for their eyesight to adjust to its colossal bulk. The snout of the creature was as long as that of an alligator. Instead of the appearance of an alligator, however, the snout swept upwards from the nostrils into a great beak shape. But the beak was covered with deeply wrinkled grey skin. The eyes above this fearsome snout were like two great glowing furnaces. From the enormous nostrils dark columns of greasy smoke belched skywards. Two enormous dragon-like wings draped the sides of the granite cliffs. But the creature was not dragon. Its form, despite the hideous face and wings, was distinctly human. Enormous human muscles rippled and bulged in its gigantic arms and legs. The creature seemed to be

trying to slake an insatiable thirst with the river, which poured into its mouth.

"When will it go away?" whispered Tansy.

Moonlight placed his finger to his lips, and they crouched behind cover to watch. The ogre drank steadily on and on.

"Surely he will have drunk enough soon!" Almost as if he had heard the words she spoke, the ogre raised its head for a moment. They heard it groan.

"The fire! The fire! Still the fire burns!"

Suddenly the cliffs shook as if with an earthquake. They saw that the ogre's great arms were fixed by mighty iron rings to the solid rock, and although he strained his sinews, and shook the very cliffs, he could not get free.

"I don't think that he will ever finish," whispered Moonlight.

"See how he is chained . . . he will go on drinking and drinking forever."

Tansy shuddered. "It is all over then . . . we must go back." As she said the words, the thread on her bracelet suddenly tightened and tugged at her leg.

Moonlight seized her arm. "We cannot go back."

"Well, we can't stay here . . . what shall we do?"

Suddenly Moonlight made up his mind. He stepped forward out of hiding. "Can you hear me?" he called aloud.

The ogre raised his fearsome head and uttered a

roar. Flame leaped seventy feet high from his nostrils.

"I hear you!" he thundered.

"Where is the fountain of life?"

The ogre uttered a laugh which echoed among the iron-grey cliffs like the thundering of an avalanche of stones. "Perhaps I know. And perhaps I do not know."

"How can I find the fountain?"

The ogre opened his gaping jaws in a hideous grin. Moonlight could see row upon row of grisly teeth.

"Come and see!" he invited jeeringly.

"Will you bite me if I come?"

"Of course . . . of course . . . how should I feed myself otherwise? Many come this way seeking the fountain of life—the brave taste good!"

Moonlight stooped to speak to Tansy. "Perhaps you can fly to the fountain . . . but I must dare the ogre. There is no other way."

"But you will be chewed in pieces."

Moonlight nodded. "Yes, I know . . . but it is the only way. The ogre is the last enemy."

Tansy's face was pale and her body trembled. "Then I will come with you."

"But you can fly."

Tansy shook her head. "If the river flows into his mouth, my wings cannot help me."

"But you do not need to come."

"Yes, I must meet Dawnstar."

Hand in hand, they walked towards a flat rock which hung over the river.

"Are you sure there is a fountain of life?" Tansy asked tremblingly.

"Yes." Moonlight replied in a steady solemn voice. "I am sure. Do you believe, Tansy?"

"Yes, I do."

"Let's go then."

Together they leaped into the swirling river and were swept down towards the gaping jaw of the ogre. As he saw them coming, a great purple tongue came out from his lips which he began to lick hungrily.

In his damp tunnel, Grood began to pull in his line. He knew that the fairy and the elf must have reached the ogre by now. One sight of the ogre would be enough to make them glad to return to him.

With his front paws he pulled the lines in, and let them fall in two heaps on the ground. He worked hard. The heaps in front of him grew larger and larger. He began to talk to himself. "Just a little more, and another bit more. Soon my slaves will come back to me. Come along my beauties! Come to dear old Grood. How I will make you work in my mines. How the Goblins will beat you with their truncheons."

From the slight resistance he felt, Grood guessed that the disconsolate pair were walking sadly back to him. A few more feet of line and he would have them.

Suddenly he uttered a shriek of rage.

At the end of the two lines were two bracelets! As if impelled by some deep magic the two bracelets slipped back on to his paws. He started backwards, but try as he would he could not shake them off. Gnashing his teeth, and slobbering with fury, he plunged wildly into the darkness of the cavern.

As the rushing waters tossed them nearer and nearer the ogre, whose mouth was gaping like a gigantic cave, a strange thing happened to Moonlight and Tansy. Far from feeling frightened, they found themselves laughing, and were filled with the sort of surging excitement that you enjoy on a fast ride at the funfair, or when taking off in an aeroplane for the very first time.

As the dark walls of the cave blotted out the sky above them, Moonlight and Tansy thought they heard a familiar, tinkling and joyful laughter in reply to their own. "Dawnstar's here!" spluttered Moonlight, just as the tumbling waters cascaded over them and the sucking current pulled them down deeper and deeper into the dark, still waters.

After what had seemed like a deep sleep, consciousness returned to Moonlight. Quickly he was wide awake, and was bubbling with excitement. He found himself lying in a great white flower. Its petals swept upwards and the light shone through them so that they glowed like a golden crocus caught in the rays of the spring sunshine. Pulling himself up to his feet and holding a yellow stamen to support himself, he stared over the top of the petals. He found that he was in the middle of a great water lily. It was floating upon the surface of an immense and beautiful blue lagoon. The lily was drifting along, pulled by a gentle current. Then Moonlight saw another lily close at hand, and peeping over the top was Tansy. She waved to him delightedly. Her face looked prettier than ever. Spreading her wings she flew to join Moonlight in his flower.

"Moonlight! Where are we?"

"I don't know . . . but look at that!"

At the far end of the lagoon was a waterfall, which glittered like diamonds as it splashed over the smooth rocks. But there was something strange about it. The water was leaping upwards, not down. The current grew faster as they were swept towards it.

"Are we dreaming?" Tansy could not believe her eyes.

"Well if so, we are dreaming together."

Suddenly they were swept into the fall, and the lily was caught in the upward rush. It was exhilarating. They shrieked in pure delight. The water foamed and swirled and gushed, but they were carried higher and higher.

Then they were in another great lagoon. Here the water was a delicate pink. For a while they drifted, and then they were caught in another gushing waterfall, and carried upwards into another lagoon. Here the water glowed a deep turquoise as though there were lights beneath the surface.

"How lovely and fresh the air smells," sighed Tansy.

Still the lily bloom drifted on till it was swept upwards again and again through the magical and multi-coloured falls. Each of them knew without anything being said that they were getting nearer and nearer to the fountain of life. A great eagerness seized them. But they were not afraid; it was a kind of longing to be home. They did not speak or even laugh now . . . there did not seem to be anything that they could say. Then Tansy gave a cry, "Look Moonlight! Look!"

"Why it's Mr Carer and Poddle."

Indeed it was. They were floating in another water lily flower quite close to them, and waved cheerily.

"If only I could fly," sighed Moonlight, "we could join them."

"Try Moonlight," Tansy whispered, "try."

Then Moonlight found that he could fly. His wings were there again; better than ever, strong and

fine. With a laugh that was almost a cry he spread his wings and circled upwards. Tansy joined him, and they danced ecstatically in the golden rays of sunlight. Then they glided down to Mr Carer and Poddle.

Before they had time to do more than hug one another in greeting they were swept upwards into the glittering silver lagoon from which sprang upwards the dazzling fountain of life.

All was too beautiful for words. There was light, and music and gladness, and standing on a platform of rock which seemed to be hewn out of gold, they saw a familiar figure. Now majestic in the finest clothes and royal robe and crown, it was unmistakably the elf who had been bruised and badly beaten in the goblin mines.

"Dawnstar, Dawnstar!" cried Moonlight and Tansy together, as the lily brought them to him, and as his hands reached down to lift them on to the rock.

"Come, my friends," said the Prince, "my Father is waiting to welcome you."

Tansy offered her ring back to Dawnstar, and he showed her the place where her tiny ruby fitted into his crown. Then Dawnstar took Moonlight's ruby and showed him where it fitted into the tip of his sceptre, and there it gleamed with hidden fires. In return Dawnstar gave them two crowns of gold studded wth gems. Mr Carer and Poddle also received crowns. Poddle had the loveliest of all. His face had grown much more noble now they had reached the top of the fountain. Wearing his crown he looked truly royal, which made Moonlight and Tansy very glad.

Then the light grew even more brilliant, more beautiful than any dawn they had ever seen in the glade. They were swept up beyond the fountain of life and into Dawnstar's kingdom, and then to the sound of splendid trumpet fanfares, higher still to meet his Father.

They were home. The ogre could not hurt them any more . . . and they were free from the bracelet of Grood forever.

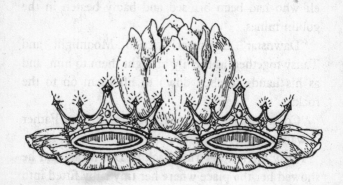

If you wish to receive *regular information* about *new books*, please send your name and address to:

London Bible Warehouse
PO Box 123
Basingstoke
Hants RG23 7NL

Name...

Address ....

....

....

....

I am especially interested in:
☐ Biographies
☐ Fiction
☐ Christian living
☐ Issue related books
☐ Academic books
☐ Bible study aids
☐ Children's books
☐ Music
☐ Other subjects

P.S. If you have ideas for new Christian Books or other products, please write to us too!